moonrise

moonrise

a collection of dreams and nightmares

neha kat

for little neha-
you were right, hearts do grow from the ground

what time is it?

dusk to afterhours

foreword

I cannot explain how fluttery I feel at this moment because you are holding moonrise in your hands and reading it within the intimate spaces of your mind. I carefully created these images in my head so that they could play out in yours, even if they show up a little differently. Thank you for letting this be a part of your daybreak, afternoon, dusk, or afterhours.

These stories took me years to collect and write in the way they were meant to be. I have been wanting to show you these stories for a long, long time. It is not a coincidence that you are reading this right now because I wrote this secretly just for you. You, reading my stories, is a dream—the kind of dreams I have when the moon rises.

Sometimes, I think of my stories as a collection of nightmares, though—because I have more nightmares than dreams, and sometimes, when the moon rises, you have nightmares instead of dreams.

Many people tried to give me advice about my nightmares—the dreaded place I go to often. The only advice that stuck with me was from someone very special to me who does not remember me anymore. It was to always create my own endings when I did not like the one given to me. This is a collection of some of my own endings because I've written so many that it feels like the beginning.

moonrise is a collection of individual stories that take you to different times and places through dreams and nightmares. Although all the stories are different and messy, moonrise is about what it's like to feel out of place, lost, and uncomfortable in the spaces of your own mind and outside of it.

trigger warning

This book contains metaphorical references to a*use, an*iety, d*pression, sui*de and g*narational tr*uma.

daybreak to
afternoon

grey umbrella

We are both on the same bus, and it won't stop raining this morning. I don't know you, but you're sitting across from me.

It's a beautiful rainy Thursday, the type that makes you feel beautiful too for walking in it. I hate holding umbrellas, but I couldn't get away with running through these heavy showers without one today. I am listening to music, and it feels intimate because only I can hear it and it's solely my experience.

I'm pretty sure I feel you looking at me, even though my nose and lips are covered. I glance at you for a split second to check, and you look away. I'm closing my eyes, taking in my music again, but making it a little softer so it blends into the rain outside.

A few minutes pass, and I feel you glancing at me again. You're making me self-conscious, so I start fiddling my thumbs, my eyes fixated on them.

From the corner of my eye, I see your water bottle fall, and I feel like you did it on purpose. Maybe because you wanted to get my attention? It rolls towards me, so I pick it up and hand it back to you. You seem pleased, like your innocent plan fell into place and I had no idea.

You thank me, and then you look into my eyes for a lengthy second. I smile at you, and I know that you feel it, even though

3

my face is covered. It was so sweet and innocent, and it felt inspired by the sweet jazz and the rain blending into my ears. I'm thinking about how you probably dropped it on purpose, and it makes me smile, even though I woke up agonized earlier today.

Eventually, it's time to get off. It's my stop first, and I get up and accidentally drop my umbrella. I'm blushing and embarrassed because what if you think I did this to get *your* attention? Or even worse—what if you never dropped your bottle to get my attention? That feeling was too sweet to not be intentional, though.

You hand me my grey umbrella now, and I thank you this time. We are looking at each other, and I know that you're smiling. I feel it, even though your face is covered. I get off the bus and almost stumble opening my grey umbrella because I am lost in thought.

This purity, this feeling of being warmly embarrassed, fueled me on this rainy, cold morning in September.

fifth or sixth avenue

City air is light in the morning until it turns thick. The buildings are bright and filled with promise until they are dim. That is why the city where certain dreams come true is the same place where certain realities strike harder. It's on the same numbered street where the dreamers swiftly walk to get past the weepers who are clinging on, lying on the same numbered street that reflects a metaphor of pain. The city is dreamy and swift to the ones who walk but slow and dreary to the ones who have no surface to walk upon.

My fortune allows me to disappear into the swift walk of the city, to drown in a blend of bliss and busyness that blinds me from the weepers below. But today, I decided to get to know the surface I walk upon every day, and pay attention to those who sit instead of walk. Focusing my attention on them made me feel this sharp pang of guilt that sat for a while. My eyes have this sensation where I am unable to cry, but they carry a numb, glazed look in them. The type of pain where keeping your eyes open has a certain hurt but closing them hurts even harder.

There are many weepers in this street, and I was taught to be wary. Wary of their anger against this world that was a dream slate to many while others had to justify their survival in the same place. I continue to keep my eyes open to avoid the excruciating pain of closing them in ignorance as I had been taught to do. My eyes glide, the dream in them fading away until I land on you.

You're sitting near a curb at the end of the numbered street. Your hair is tousled, your hand over your head. Your eyes struck me because they had the same dream in them that I was losing just by looking at your reality.

Then, I see him beside you.

Your other hand, the one not lost in disarray in your delicate hair, rests on top of your dog. He has more hope in his eyes than you. He seems stronger than you. His tail wags when he notices that I am walking towards you. I notice a couple of paper scraps and a few broken pencils around you, all with blunt tips.

You're an artist, I can tell. I want to sit by you and give each of your sketches the type of undivided attention they are effortlessly aching for. Learn about you and how the world hurt you. I want to learn the story behind your sketches. Your striking eyes made me choose *you* to be intrigued by, not anyone else in the city today.

You ask for food or money, and I wish I had cash to give you. I was not wary of you, though. I was more sure about you than any of the people that I am close to. I remember I had a few crackers in a package, and I handed you them with a smile. I hope you saw the light in my eyes for you. You bless me, and that energy has been fueling me ever since. I am going to dream on this numbered street for you and for me now.

I get up from kneeling beside you and start walking against the path again. I am a few blocks away now, and I turn back to see you, the city air thick against my hair. I look for you and see you carefully open my crackers, and you break them with your artist hands and slowly feed them to your dog.

I have this trust for you, and even though I have only known you for this morning, I know that my trust for you is whole. I find myself in a corner store, buying a loaf of bread, a little bag of dog treats and some sharpened pencils.

I walk back to fifth or sixth avenue, whichever one you were sitting at before. Your dog's tail starts to wag again in excitement, and I get excited too, because I know these pencils will be blunt soon.

I don't feel wary when I am with you.

violet velvet

Even though people come and leave my house often, only I know about all the trinkets I store in there. I have a lot of trinkets, especially in my own room—some that are new and others that have been with me since I was young. I store them all around, some of them out in the open so that maybe visitors notice. I don't think they do, or maybe they do and don't want to bring it up. The deeper trinkets I usually hide in the liminal spaces of my room. I wish I could clean them out sometimes, especially the hidden ones.

No matter how hard I try, I cannot give up any of them— even the hidden ones because they are special in this twisted way. It feels like no one has noticed my special trinkets, and I am sure of it because sometimes I visit their houses, but the trinkets I have do not seem to be there. I know all of these trinkets well, but sometimes I question whether I am supposed to bring them to the front of my house, and other times I wonder if I actually know what they are and what I can use them for.

Lately, I feel like sharing my special trinkets with someone else. Or bring them over to a friend's house just so I can see them in a new place. My house is decorated in a consistent palette of off-whites and light nudes. These trinkets are all different colors though, and sometimes it feels like the trinkets are clashing against my house in a frightening, stark contrast. I want to keep them, but they do not look the best here, in my house.

I decided to gather all my strength and lug these trinkets out of my house so I could show my friends. Maybe it would look better in their eyes, in their house. Luckily, my whole street is filled with friends of mine, some that I met four months ago, some that I met six years ago. I have tried bringing my trinkets out before, but I never knew which house they would be the most welcome in. I never knew which of my golden-hearted friends would be the most interested in looking at my trinkets or, more importantly, getting to know how I got them.

Even though imagining which house to take my trinkets to usually stopped me, I decided that today I would walk through my street and figure out which house felt the best to walk into. I did not want to be walking the streets at night though, so I waited until daybreak to start packing my trinkets. They were heavy to carry, especially on my back while I walked the streets, so I wanted to make them as compact as possible.

I have several violet-colored velvet drawstring bags in the back of my closet. One by one, while the sun comes up, I put each trinket into a bag of its own. I tug at the drawstrings to close each one until I have a pile of all my trinkets that clash with my own house. I place them in a pile in front of the window and watch the sun lay its rays on them. I looked at the neighborhood, trying to imagine finally opening these trinkets, for the first time, in someone else's house. It would probably still clash with their house, but hopefully less.

Before I put my walking shoes on, I thought about it over again because I have always loved my house, even with all the troubling, colorful trinkets in it. It just felt almost like these trinkets had a gravitational pull towards my house like they only wanted to stay in here and never go anywhere else.

I've spent most of my time in my house because I like people coming in and out of it. I found it slightly harder to enter someone else's door, even though they usually opened them for me to walk through. I put these thoughts aside though, and I carried all the violet velvet bags with me and started walking along the street. I need to find the right house and the right doors to lug my trinkets through.

After a couple of houses, I went into the house of a new friend—I thought showing him would be easier since he seemed so welcoming. When I first showed him the trinkets, he did not quite understand, but he accepted them. So, whenever I felt like my trinkets were clashing with the walls of my own house, I brought them over to him for a little while.

We would drink tea together, I would tear up often when I talk about how these trinkets came to be in my possession, and he tears up showing me the trinkets he has and isn't proud of. One day, I brought a trinket, encased in violet velvet, into his house, but as soon as I unwrapped it, my friend went into a dreadful silence.

The silence felt like this pause, one that I could not understand. It felt like he finally noticed how ugly my trinket was, and he did not want me to bring it over anymore. He would never directly push me through his doors, but his silence led me to push myself through them.

Now I am back on the streets, and it's raining outside. The velvet bags I am lugging around suddenly feel infinite, and there are water droplets rolling off them. At first, I thought his silence was because of how ugly and colorful my trinkets were, and it made my mind feel heavy. After lying in my house and my mind for a week though, I realized that I had probably just gone to the wrong house—one where my trinket was not actually welcome.

A few mornings after that, I finally gained the courage to put the trinkets on my back again, in these violet velvet bags. I needed to find a space to bring them to. I think that this time I am going to really contemplate which house I walk into today, maybe a more familiar friend I have known for longer. As I walk the street again, I find another house, just as welcoming as the one before. However, I have visited my friend in this house before, and I knew the interior was different from the previous house I walked through.

My friend opens her arms to embrace me after I walk through her doors, and she notices my violet velvet bags, even before I mention them. She opens one herself, and I think that she might understand its twisted beauty. She takes it out of the bag entirely and displays it at the very front of her inviting home. This was the same trinket that my newer friend probably thought was ugly, and it comforts me to know that it was not actually about the trinket, it was actually the person I chose to show it to.

The comfort I felt here was probably the closest I have ever felt to my own home, so I bring my trinkets here often. She opens them so delicately and takes the time to understand them through my storytelling of how they came to be with me. It seems like I could show her any of my trinkets in the way that she loves showing me hers. She would always find a place for them in her home, usually at the front.

I think a part of me was forever insecure about my trinkets though, when I remembered how my newer friend could not even respond to them. So one day, to validate my insecurity,

I wrapped my biggest trinket hidden in my house in the same violet velvet bag. It felt extra heavy, but I dragged it to her house anyway.

She seemed more restless than usual and tugged at the drawstrings. She tugged harder and harder because it was hard to open. She got frustrated and threw the violet velvet bag across her living room. The bag still did not open, but it horrifically shattered and made this noise I would never forget.

Without saying another word, I apologized and picked up the broken trinket, its pieces floating around aimlessly in the bag. I walked through her doors and dragged the bag back to my house. It seemed heavier than earlier today when I was lugging it to my friend's house before it had shattered.

I walk through my own doors, and I easily open the drawstrings on the violet velvet bag with the broken trinket. I look at what is left of it and wonder why it was so hard to get to.

I look up and around me and notice that the walls of my house have started to break from the inside, and they bend towards the middle like they are going to collapse soon.

half and half

We both like coffee, but I never thought I would eventually become his half and half. I already learned my lesson the first time and this was not supposed to happen to me again.

When I wake up, I think of everything as dreams and nightmares. Dreams are anything I want to keep close to me because they are special and come few and far between. Nightmares are anything I want to release, and sometimes it feels like these things have a way of always finding me when I feel like I can't handle it.

When you try to hold onto something, or when you try to keep it in a box, it moves even further away. Nightmares are not light and airy like dreams—nobody tries to hold onto them. When I wake up from a nightmare, I try to capture it within my palms and throw it out my window. Specifically, outside my window, outside my room, outside my space, outside my mind. The nightmare ends up sticking to my palms, unable to leave me. I think that might be why my dreams are so hard to hold onto and feel far away, but my nightmares stay to follow me wherever I go.

I already learned my lesson the first time, when I opened up the darkest and lightest depths of me, and let go of my pride, my dream. I confessed to someone that I liked them, only for them to tell me they were confused about me. I felt like half and half, sometimes deserving of love, sometimes not really. I decided after that to keep my depth a little deeper. I started drinking my coffee a little darker too, because I learned I am not supposed to be anyone's half and half. So when I liked someone new, I was very careful and cautious. I wanted to get rid of the feeling and keep drinking my coffee bold and dark. I tried to hold on to my pride—I tried to keep it in a box. Just like my dreams, it felt like it was getting further away.

Eventually, I decided to compress it with my hands, and it felt even smaller and tighter than usual. Since we spent the morning together, and since I know how he likes his coffee, I decided to make him a cup. I hate to say it because it pulls at my pride, but I know how much milk and sugar he likes in it.

This morning, though, I was running really low on everything—milk, patience, coffee grounds, pride, sugar, and hope. I had to gather everything I had left to make him his cup. Now I barely had anything left, because I poured everything I had in my kitchen and my heart into a cup, making sure it was exactly the way he liked it. None left for me, and nobody would even think of making me some. This coffee had a faint touch of chicory in it, a little milk, and exactly two spoons of sugar. My kitchen and I were empty now—not much hope, no sugar, no pride, no coffee, no patience, and no milk.

I have an odd feeling inside, the kind that I get when my nightmares are stuck compressed to my palms after I hurt my arms trying to throw them. My legs are sore too, but I walk over to him anyway to hand over the coffee I made for him. He seemed happy, and I felt empty like his coffee cup was about to be. He finishes it, and I look at my empty cup, then my empty kitchen with no coffee ingredients.

14

He inhales carefully and starts telling me that I am half and half to him, too. He says he likes me sometimes, but other times not really. He is confused about me, unsure about me, and I wonder if it is because my dwindling coffee ingredients were not enough for him.

I thought about how I wanted coffee that morning but decided I only had enough for his cup. I thought about how my worst nightmare—becoming yet another person's half and half—had stayed to follow me. It must have stuck to my palms when I tried to throw it out. I knew in the darkest, deepest part of me that he would not have ever made me a coffee and that he did not know how I like mine—no sugar, a little oat milk, and a touch of caramel.

I knew that the entire time, which is why this was not supposed to happen to me again.

ecru pages

Bookstores feel like sanctuaries to me even though I do not go often enough. It feels different from going to other places because I go downtown and to coffee shops to meet other people, but I go to bookstores to get to know myself better. When I do go into a bookstore, I don't pay any attention to anyone else around me because they are probably busy connecting with themselves, too.

I think a couple of months ago I decided that I needed to pay attention to myself a little more than I usually do, so I decided to try and go to a bookstore every Saturday morning. I had been reading this book that I picked because of the way the cover made me feel. This dark cover with golden trim, and the thick pages were ecru inside.

When I started reading it, it became clear that the characters were written by a woman. The descriptions were vividly emotional and the characters cared for each other so much that it had to have been real. It was hard to get through because I wanted to melt in all the details and remember them for a long time. I read it every Saturday at this one table in a dark corner of the store that not many people knew about.

One of those Saturdays, I noticed a dark-haired, shy-eyed man at one of the tables in my corner, and we exchanged friendly smiles. I noticed he would be there every Saturday, at the same time, reading his own book. The pages of his book were the same comforting shade of ecru that mine were, but he laid his book flat on the table when he read so I could not tell what it was.

A couple of Saturdays passed, and I think I might like him. Not anything too deep, but his smile was inviting and I wanted to get to know him better. The thing is though, every time I look at him, I remember when I met someone else at my regular coffee shop in the same way. It started with the same shy eyes and inviting smile but lighter hair. The light-haired man finally said hey and our initial exchange about coffee effortlessly turned into talking about music because we had the same taste.

Somewhere in there, the coffee shop run-ins and light conversations turned into long walks at the park where we talked about what our heaviest baggage was or our biggest fears. Somewhere in there, I broke my own rules and fell for the idea. I was convinced it would work out, but one night, when we were lying on our backs side by side at the park, he told me that he would only ever want to quickly kiss my lips, never slowly kiss my face or gently push my hair to the side. If I had to guess, he liked me but not enough—I am tired of guessing, anyway. The devastation lasted longer than I wanted it to, but the idea of him eventually dissipated as he did.

I tried to promise myself that I was not going to fall for shy eyes ever again, especially not until I found someone who wanted to get to know my heart too. I think that's why on these Saturdays, every time I want to finally just say hello to the dark-haired man of ecru pages, I compare him to the shy eyes I knew before. I know it is twisted and unfair but that is where my mind goes after my first devastation.

17

The whole story with the dark-haired man feels like it was written by a woman, but my first one kind of did, too. The smile feels genuine like maybe he would eventually like my face as much as the rest of me, but my first one did, too. The way he looked at me the same way every Saturday morning at the same time with those shy eyes, my first story was kind of like that, too. I did want to know who he was, and what he was reading, but I feel like the risk of the shy eyes was not worth it because of what happened before.

Another few Saturdays pass, and this time, the man of ecru pages comes and sits next to me instead of at his own table. There was no chair across from me, so he slid into the one next to me. He finally says hello, but when he's right next to me, I hear my first story again, the one that I had to slowly unlearn because it stained me permanently.

I got up and left the bookstore because it didn't feel like my sanctuary anymore. I thought about it all week, and even though he was technically a stranger, I could not stop thinking about it because I wanted to get to know him all along. I was just scared. I decided to break my promise to myself—because I want to read those ecru pages.

Hoping he came in this Saturday, I walked in. He's sitting at his usual spot. There is a chair across from him, but I bring it over to his side and sit next to him.

He finally lifted up the book so I could see what these ecru pages were, and I noticed it was the same book I was reading.

coffee cake in november

The coffee cake I bake is soft and cinnamon-traced, and the espresso I pour is dark and rich like my introversion. I always have both ready at my bakery, but I only have one regular who orders them as a pairing.

Every morning when I am wearing my batter-stained apron behind my counter, I feel a warm bliss when I remember that I have regulars. People who order the same thing because they have love and trust for something I created by hand, and they want to experience it again and again.

I try not to say much at the bakery and just hold onto the warm feelings of watching people form connections with one another over my desserts. I have been waiting all Fall for someone to get my favorite pairing, and two weeks ago, you did. You seemed like you were in a rush, so I put the coffee cake in its paper wrapping. When I handed it to you, you smiled and rushed out my door.

I glance outside my window and notice you taking the coffee cake out of its wrapping to take a bite. I smile when you close your eyes while you eat it in the cold. Ever since then, you come in every morning, and you eat it right outside the door a few minutes later. Last week, I started asking you, "Coffee cake, right?" and you smiled in return.

One day, you came in with tear-stained eyes and something missing from your usual expression. I brought you your usual and added an extra piece. This week, I have the middle piece cut and ready for you every morning before you come in. Every morning, you unwrap it and eat it in bliss in the wind of the Fall. It looks like you found the traces of cinnamon because you look like you feel warmer when you bite into it.

Yesterday was the first day this November you did not come in, and I felt a strange hollowness inside where my warm bliss usually is. I wonder if your tear stains are back, you forgot to stop by, or maybe you finally caught a cold.

I took the coffee cake I saved for you and walked outside after a few hours of waiting. I ate it like you usually do, eyes closed and in the cold November air. I feel a slight pain, like I should not have gotten used to this pattern, and it was foolish to prepare something before someone even came. I know better than to depend on empty recurrences for my inner bliss or get used to patterns—even if they feel consistent and comfortable.

So today on this November morning, I try not to look for you. I baked a fresh coffee cake, soft and cinnamon-traced like every morning, but I did not cut your middle piece for you today.

A few minutes later, though, you walk in through the door, bringing the air of Autumn with you. "For here," you say for the first time.

So I smile and walk over to the coffee cake I just baked and place the middle piece on a plate.

crimson mittens

On this January or February morning, I was only five years old and it was snowing outside. I was standing on my tiptoes, my nose almost against the window, and using my eyes to follow how the snow was slowly falling onto the pine trees.

This was my first snow, and it was new because I had only ever lived in warm places before. It was bitterly cold outside, the kind that stings sharply if your skin is not fully covered. I was ready for school, wearing a puffy pink and purple snowsuit and excited to touch the flurries when we got to play outside. I followed my mother outside the apartment, into the car and watched as she poured warm water over the frozen windows to loosen the thin layer of ice. She drove through the falling snow, and before I hopped out of the car, she handed me two things.

One was a little plastic bag with two baby carrots in it so that I could put noses on the snowmen I was about to build. The other was a pair of her own beautiful crimson mittens since I did not like my own. She slipped them over my hands, and even though they were too big on me, I knew they were special. She told me to take good care of them, and then she drove back home.

At playtime that day, we went out into the snow, and I ran

into it. I built a clumsy snowman, but he looked majestic once I pressed his baby carrot nose in. I wanted to find sticks for his arms, so I ran to look for them, but I fell down into the snow. When I picked myself up, I found the sticks I wanted and went back to my clumsy snowman. As I stuck his arms in, I realized that my own arms were in pain, the type of pain that stings sharply if your skin is not fully covered. I looked down and realized that I had lost my crimson mittens—the special ones that my mom had given to me to keep my hands warm.

I remember feeling a deep guilt inside for the first time, running through the snow hoping to see little red mittens somewhere in the white. All I could think about was how cold my mother's hands were because she had given me her own special crimson mittens.

My teacher wonders why I was scurrying through the snow, searching intensely for crimson. I explained to her what I had lost and how, now that they were gone, I was not sure I could handle it unless they came back to me.

A few days later, my teacher showed me a pair of crimson mittens she had found close by and asked me if they were the ones I had lost. I glance at them, and they look exactly like my mother's special mittens I had lost. I was going to take them back, but then my mind wandered a little bit.

I had already forgotten exactly what my mother's crimson mittens had looked like, and I imagined how sad another girl would be if these were her mittens and I was about to take them. So I told her I did not think they were my mittens, even though I realized later that they were.

I think about that January or February morning every winter, even after fifteen years. Not only did I lose something that was dangerously special and warm to me, but it made its way back

22

to me and I lost it again.

It reminds me of how last year, I met your warmth when I felt cold and lost, and I thought you were given to me like those mittens were. When we decided to split ways on a cold January morning, I did not forget how special you were, but I was forgetting how special I was. We decided to never talk again because I needed to learn how to face the cold on my own.

Even though it has been months since then, sometimes, when I feel a sharp sting, I run through the fields, hoping to see a little crimson somewhere in the white.

It does not cross my mind too often anymore, but when it does I know that if you ever found your way back to me, I would not let you go—the way I let go of my crimson mittens.

yellow memories

The center of my lips is always a little bit swollen, and there are always scars on the bottom where they meet my teeth. Once I start thinking about how hurt my lips are, I cannot stop thinking about how uncomfortable my whole mouth is. The way my lips are always being bitten by the teeth they lay in front of just feels natural because I can barely remember a time when I was fully comfortable with the way my lips felt on my face and in front of my teeth.

Oftentimes I want out of my teeth, my mouth, my face. It feels like I am not in my body, or I am trapped in it and cannot get out. When I was much, much younger, though, I remember my lips were bright and unbroken. My mouth was pretty much the same as it is now, but back then, I guess I never took the time to realize how uncomfortable my lips and teeth felt. Sometimes I want to go back in time and be blissfully unaware of the little things that make me uncomfortable in myself, on myself, or outside of myself. Sometimes I want to go back in time so that I can notice or feel things for the very first time again.

Every time I think about when I was younger, the memory has a shiny yellow lining around it. One of my most yellow memories was meeting my first butterfly. I had only seen pictures of them in a book, and I wanted one to sit on my finger like the little girl on the cover.

I do not remember what trip it was that I met my first butterfly, but it was one of those family road trips where you stop every couple of hours to take in the view and stretch your legs out a little. In the middle of the stops, we came to a field that, because of my height at the time, seemed endless. Some short shrubs and plants would brush against my little legs, and I do not remember it being uncomfortable at the time. I saw a single butterfly, orangey with white speckles, fluttering around in the orangey-tinted sky around us.

I ran through the grass with my right hand sticking out in case the butterfly wanted to rest atop my skin the way I wanted. I ran until I lost my breath and eventually fell to the ground trying to chase my first butterfly. I bled from both my knees, and the scars from my raised skin would stay there on me forever. I started crying because I felt embarrassed and regretful trying to chase it. The scars on my knees remind me of butterfly wings, partly because they look the same on both sides and partly because I know now never to chase my yellow memories again because it feels uncomfortable.

A few weeks ago, I walked out of my local coffee shop after finishing a couple of unfinished stories. I felt satisfied because it had taken me a while to give my stories their endings. When I walked out, a man was standing next to my car, talking to a friend of his. He asked me if I had a good day, and I smiled before starting to answer. While I told him how my day went, a single butterfly, orangey with white speckles on it, flew in our vicinity.

Remembering my yellow memories, I folded my arms behind my back, letting my hands wrap around each other because I no longer chase after future scars. I'm suddenly very aware of the scars on my knees that are decades faded.

The butterfly fluttered by my nose and flew in an intimate circle around me twice. I followed it delicately, but only with a gentle stare. It flew behind me, but just when I thought it had flown away from me, it sat on my pointer finger on my right hand. I carefully separated my hands and brought my arms to the front again, and the butterfly still sat on my finger. It stayed there for a couple of seconds like it wanted to be there with me, and it flew away.

It felt like I had just made another yellow memory. The man tells me it is good luck and I laugh before I tell him to have a good afternoon.

I sat in my car, thinking about my new yellow memory, and forgot for a moment about the scars on my swollen lips.

champagne charmeuse

My sister stitches, and I buy her fabric. We moved to a sleepy town about a year ago, and now we finally have the peaceful Sundays we always wanted growing up. Today is a peaceful Sunday morning, and I am walking through the calm sidewalks with my sister. She carries a navy and forest green tote bag, her signature piece.

I am wearing a flowy sundress that does not take my shape. I can feel the light air against my thighs and the sun gleaming against my shoulders. There are many little shops alongside the sidewalk, and my sister and I still stop to look at almost all of them, even a year later. She is looking for a new fabric, one that she can use to stitch me a new dress.

We finally stumble upon a shop with velvets and cottons in the window and open the door. It is one of those doors that reminds me of when I was younger because there is a noise of chimes as the door closes behind me, and my dress flounces around again when I feel the last gust of wind. The sun is streaming through the windows, flowing through the entire store, and we spend what seems like all morning stroking different fabrics. There are different hues and textures, but nothing feels right to her yet.

We see the silks and charmeuses lying on top of a table, aside from all the other fabrics hanging from the short ceiling. They were spread shapelessly, folding and creasing in this effortless, decadent way. It may have seemed a little scattered, but the folds gave the silks a contrast foreign to any fabric in the store. My sister and I were engulfed in every fold. The way that the champagne charmeuse, in particular, laid on the surface was bare and humble. I noticed that the shapeless fabric looked beautiful on its own, even before trying to take the shape of what was under it. I lay three fingers against the champagne-colored silk, and my sister takes it to the counter, her tote bag hitting her side as she walks.

We walk home, the champagne charmeuse effortlessly spilling out of my sister's tote bag. My sister lays her scissors and pins atop the champagne folds, ready to put her craft into the silks.

I bake us a loaf of bread and when I take it out, there's still steam rising from it. My sister is sitting at the dining table, her hands against the sewing machine. I put the loaf on the table and sit next to her. We spend the afternoon daydreaming, eating bread, and laughing, the light in the windows growing brighter. I almost forget how agitating our Sundays used to be long ago. Eventually, it is a couple afternoons later, and my sister holds up the dress of champagne charmeuse, her eyes filled with calm and sparkle.

I slip into my new dress, noticing how the champagne charmeuse lays stunningly against my skin and takes my shape.

journal at the bodega

When I was a few feet shorter and a lot less wise, I had a teacher who would take us to the library once a week. I would always choose a book, reading it cover to cover a couple of times before it was time to get a new one.

One week, I chose a small book that was a little larger than both my palms put together that had thick pages inside. It had a vintage sketch of a flower stand on the outside, and I wanted to know the story behind the cover.

After I checked the book out, I opened the book up and was severely disappointed. Inside the book were beautiful sketches—of people, of flowers, and two holding hands throughout. The only thing missing were the words—I had picked a book with no words. I was confused and upset because I had never seen a book without a story, so I asked my teacher what the problem was with the book.

She told me it was because I had to come up with my own story in the empty spaces, something I had never really done before. I realized it was me who had to give the book its story, so I took a pencil and filled the empty spaces of the book with what I thought the story was.

I wrote about a girl who bought the flowers at the flower stand and how she found a friend to share them with by the end of the story. When it came time to return the book, I had to erase my story, but it always stuck with me even though it did not stick to the pages.

Ever since then, I wrote my own stories often, especially for pictures I did not understand at first.

A couple of mornings ago, I went to my favorite bodega on the corner of my street as soon as it opened. It always has rows of florals, some of them rich and some of them bright, and it always takes me back to the very first story I had made up.

My teacher gave me empty spaces to write in, and it taught me about myself and the world around me. I wanted to pass that gift along, neighborhood by neighborhood. So when I woke up today, I drew a picture of my favorite flower bodega on the cover of an off-white journal. I found the first page and wrote in black ink, "What's the weather like inside of you today?" and left the pen between the journal pages.

I walked over to the bodega and left the journal between a couple of vibrant bouquets, hoping that someone would give my journal a story. I left with a bouquet of pale roses that had baby's breath and moonflowers sprinkled throughout.

This morning I went back to the bodega for my journal and now empty pen, and I am going to spend the rest of the day learning the stories behind my cover.

I read about the sunshine, flurries, and thunderstorms inside of people who frequented the bodega and smiled when I realized they had all come up with their own stories in the empty spaces I had left for them.

blueberry tart

I had to set my alarm hours earlier than usual this morning, but it was not hard to open my eyes today. I had been waiting to go blueberry picking for months, and the farms around me were finally in bloom. I had brought several empty baskets to fill because I was determined to fight through the blazing heat to pick enough blueberries to make a tart. I walked through the bushes behind the farm, picking off a berry with my right hand and using my left hand to keep the leaves around each berry away.

I drove home, beads of sweat on my tanned skin against the baby blue sundress I was wearing. I had filled almost all four of the baskets I had brought. They were my absolute favorite fruit, and I took a moment to look at the infinite shades of blues and deep purples, with a few that were light green.

I have gotten so tired and thirsty that I feel like I need to collapse asleep or drink water endlessly. I grab one of my clear glasses from the shelf, with little square indents, and fill it from the pitcher of water I had. I drink it quicker than I ever remember drinking water before and do the same with the next three refills. I run the berries under the water in the sink and then dry them while I think about how I was about to bake them into a tart. I throw a couple of the berries into my mouth

31

and realize how tired I have gotten from the summer heat. I manage to walk upstairs to my room, mindlessly holding my empty glass. I place the glass on my dresser, right across from my bed.

I decide to nap for an hour or so. That way, I have the rest of the afternoon to bake my tart. I get under the patchwork quilt that I only use in the summer and doze off. As I drift off, I find myself in this endless garden, just looking around. It is breathtaking, and I feel like making my own bouquet from the variety of flowers all around me. It was unbelievably warm, and even the gorgeous views could not distract me from the discomfort. I tried to walk around a little, but the heat worsened, and I longed for water more and more. Wiping the beads of sweat across my forehead, I realized my throat was drying out and my head felt light and dizzy.

I notice a burning sensation start at my toes and then rise throughout my body from the inside out. Rubbing my eyes and gathering what is left of my vision, I notice little flames in a circle around me becoming bigger and bigger as I inhale. I notice that my body is burning from within, and I feel the fire run through every organ I know I have. I feel it on the outside, too. I feel the clear skin on my face blister and turn red. My face and arms become splotchy like the fire wanted to leave its mark on me.

I began to wonder how all of the flowers around me were flourishing without a single drop of water nearby. I am the only one in this field that wasn't in bloom. Everything around me seemed okay.

I know I need water—and immediately. Drinking the water and feeling it go throughout my body was the only way to remove the inner fire that did not belong inside of me. I bend down into a bed of sunflowers and notice an empty glass with little square indents in it. I realize with anger that it is completely empty. I jump in a flurry several feet ahead of me and find a desolate golden set of stairs in the middle of the field I can take.

I run down the stairs to find a pitcher filled to the top with water. I fill my glass with water and drink it as quickly as possible. I fill the pitcher again, filling my glass to the top. I run back up the stairs, but instead of the sunflowers from before, I see my bed and nightstand in the center of the field. I drink exactly half of the water I had brought with me and place the half-full glass on my nightstand, right next to my bed. I pause to think about how my skin hurts to touch and would never look the same again.

I wake up from this weird dream, and my tanned skin is covered in goosebumps on my legs, but beads of sweat on my arms. I glance outside the window I had left open, noting how the cerulean shade of the summer morning sky had turned into an intense orange sunset.

Half-conscious, I ran to my mirror to touch my face to ensure it did not actually get burnt. I feel thirsty again, so I plan on walking downstairs to fill the empty glass I had left on my dresser. I approached the dresser to get the glass, but it was not there anymore. Feeling nervous, I hesitantly look at my nightstand, and I see the half-full glass of water that I must have leaped up to get.

I find my hand covering my mouth, and I sit that way for an hour before I start kneading the crust for my blueberry tart.

my cliffhanger

They all end in the same way, with me ending. For the past five years. There were two times when they did not end with my end.

In one of them, I was running in a flouncy white dress, crying, which is a recurring scene I am too familiar with. I am unsure where I was running from, but I remember wanting to burn the sun instead of allowing it to burn me. I wanted to cry until I had formed the moon with my tears. I wanted to escape to something much greater. I think I had ended in different ways in all my dreams, and a couple of times I did it to myself, which was a lot more peaceful because I was in control.

One of these times, I was in these beautiful mountains where I found a gorgeous cliff. I remember looking around and thinking that if this beauty around me would not keep me here, nothing would. I no longer saw anything to go on for. Nobody felt like they were worth going on for, but most of all, I did not feel like I had anything to offer the beautiful world that I am from.

I remember sitting close to the edge of that gorgeous cliff—white dress under my knees and my legs pointing ninety degrees off it. Sitting on the edge of this cliff, looking down to see that I was halfway up to heaven at this height, and seeing the world I was about to leave when I glanced down was the most peace I had ever felt in my dream life.

Rather than being frightening or sending that scary jolt down my spine, it felt blissful to see the world under my feet, my feet that walked upon the world for so long. I knew that I had the will to push off and thrust forward, throwing myself up to the sky while physically landing down at the earth's feet. I was about to float away by floating downwards, completely at peace with myself and sure of the decision I was making.

This is usually the part where I become half-awake since all my dreams end this way, but I force my eyes shut to try to continue with this oddly peaceful sequence. Only this time, as I was about to thrust and fall, I felt someone run up to the edge of the cliff and grab the arm that I had stretched behind me while I let my legs dangle off the cliff.

They pulled me back onto the safe part of the cliff, which was painful because of their strength. It sent a scary jolt down my spine, but as their pulse met mine I felt the nerve in their arm when they touched me. I knew that I had to experience that jolt again and again and again and again until it was time for me to end on the earth's terms. I wanted to either save myself or end myself, either way I was at peace because that meant I owned my mind and I was in control.

But this time, it was them that kept me from thrusting forward. I saved myself because I wanted to feel them again.

I saved myself because I wanted to feel me feel them again.

afternoon to dusk

peace train

I am drowning in a place where no one understands me and no one is like me. I need to rediscover myself and come back to me because I finally realized that it is not that there is something wrong with me. It is my environment that is discouraging and uninspiring.

I am going to make a daring move that feels airy and light. I run past the streets until I reach a lofty, majestic train. The train moves at a comfortably slow pace as if it is lending a hand and reaching out to me.

I pull one hand over my hat and use the other to toss the small bag I have onto the train. I clutch my hat harder as I step inside. As soon as I get onto the peace train, I felt a wave of calm rush over me. My previously racing heart slowed down just a touch, and my muscles loosened up a little. It almost felt foreign after all the seas of doubt I had been swimming in lately.

Even though this entire journey was dangerously risky, at this moment, it felt incredibly safe. A coffee cart was moving through the middle of the train, and people's chatter about their oncoming journeys filled the silence of the air.

I am so exhausted from crying for several nights before. I sip on some chamomile tea and glance outside. The view of the toxic hometown had changed into these tall mountains, ones that reminded me of how small I was and how, eventually, I would be okay. There is greenery surrounding the scene and a soft skyline. Every sip of this tea feels like a moment I had missed in my previous life.

Eventually, I completely lose myself to the beauty of the scene in the windows, and I fall asleep. Something rustles beneath me, and with my eyes still closed, I begin to silently panic because I don't know if I can take it if this was all just a dream.

I hesitantly open my heavy eyes, and the scenery outside my window is thankfully the same, except the sky is tinted with an amber gradient, and the sun is going down. I quickly notice the entire view is sideways, and I realize I had fallen asleep on someone's shoulders and fallen into their lap.

I am not sure who it is, but I don't mind that much because I have not felt this comfortable in a long time. I slowly move my gaze to meet his eyes. His soft eyes and warm smile meet mine, and he holds onto my cheek, pushing a strand of my hair aside.

I slowly put my hand in his and find my hat upon his dark hair.

ashland

I got to pick where I would go this afternoon, and I chose my childhood bedroom. Even outside the manila-colored door, I could hear little me's laughter radiating through the room. I gently open the door and peer inside.

The pale-yellow walls lined with sparkly princess stickers and scribbles of stems and leaves with hearts atop the stems instead of flowers fill me with an overwhelming sense of longing. I look at the netted hammock in one of the corners that had all my stuffies sitting on it, including my very favorite blueberry-scented stuffed cow. There was a stand next to the bed where rows of books were stacked on top of each other, but there were even more books sprawled on the ground. A little desk with a little chair was pressed against the window and had paint bottles open on it, with a bunch of little paintings taped up on the wall near it. Little me was sitting in the little chair with hot pink paint streaks in her hair. She jumped on my back, and we lay beside each other on the little bed.

I made sure I stayed silent and heard her talk about anything and everything because I wanted to get to know her again. She tells me that she started having a couple of nightmares here and there, and it scared her sometimes. I stroked her hair, wishing I could tell her it got better with time. She tells me how she liked making up her own stories and pictures, but she did not like it when other people saw them because they would not understand them in the way she wanted. She told me she did not like how her hair curled every which way naturally, and I delicately tugged at one to show her how it bounced so beautifully and let her know that it made her so special.

Even though she did not like showing anyone her art or ideas, she pulled at my hand and ran towards the walls to show me because I made her feel safe. We go to the corner of the room and she shows me her favorite paintings. She painted an underwater scene where the fish all had hundreds of glittery rainbow scales, and they were at a tea party. She showed me another one, where it was an umbrella holding a girl instead of a girl holding an umbrella. I asked her why she drew it backward, and she told me it was because the girl was tired. I asked her why she made the sky shades of purple and pink instead of blue, and she said it made more sense because the sky made her feel warm inside. She went through fourteen paintings in a stack that were crinkly from the paint, and we walked over to the wall.

On the wall were those scribbles I first noticed. A row of stems that were all different lengths, with two little leaves, one pointing from the left side of the stem and one pointing from the right side of the stem. On top of the stems were hearts instead of flowers. I asked her about these, and she told me that love grew from the ground, and sometimes it would wilt. Some love was tall, and some love was short. Sometimes a bunch of the love was picked from the ground it belonged to and gathered into a bouquet that someone would get. At first, it would look pretty, and the person getting the bouquet would be happy about it, but it would slowly wilt eventually. The love

42

would wilt because love grows from the ground. I teared up remembering how I drew love on stems when I was younger.

She told me she did not really like talking to people because it made her understand herself and the world around her less. Drawing everything the wrong way helped her understand everything around her. She told me she knew the skies were blue, but they made her feel pink and purple inside. If she did not paint it that way, she could not understand the sky.

She has a little ring made of grass sitting on her nightstand. She explained she got married to a happy boy during recess at a dandelion-fluff and grass-ring wedding. She blushed when she said he loves her for her, the way her curly hair bounces, and because she is unique. It was the deepest feeling I had ever felt at the time. I picked up her grass ring, but it did not go past the tips of my pinky finger. I smiled, remembering my little wedding, but I did not have the heart to tell younger me that Ashland did not last past the first grade.

I thought about all the people I have met since then and how it never was as easy and open-hearted as how I felt at my kindergarten wedding with Ashland. When I told her about all these disappointments, she simply asked why it was so hard to trust love because, she said, Ashland had made her feel happy enough.

I could not answer, but I began to wonder if things had become far too complicated as I grew up. Maybe everything was supposed to be much simpler and love truly was supposed to grow from the ground.

I felt completely at peace in her room, in my room. I lay next to her again, telling her to hold on to me tighter because she felt further and further the older I grew. She tugged at my shirt and asked if she could come see my room. I took her but told her it was nowhere near as whimsical as hers.

Her eyes were bright and excited, and she took a step in. I watched her walk around and look at the painting of a blue sky and green fields I had hanging up on my wall. She told me it was very "real" looking and asked if I made it. I told her I bought it, to which she asked why we did not just draw our own. I started to talk about how I did not have time, but that seemed like a terrible explanation compared to her beautiful descriptions of her paintings. She called my decor pretty, but the light in her eyes was nowhere as bright as it was before she walked in.

She noticed some scribbles I had absentmindedly drawn on a blank notepad I kept on my desk while I was on the phone the other day. She smiled when she saw a little heart with a smiley face in the center of the scribbles, with a stem under the heart and a leaf on either side. She finally plopped on top of my bed, sinking into the blankets, and clutched onto my very favorite blueberry-scented stuffed cow I still kept. I lay beside her, falling asleep, talking about how love grows from the ground.

When I wake up, younger me is not there anymore, but she is not as far away.

your red nails

Almost every late afternoon reminds me of you, finding myself in you and us together. Ever since you let go of the earth, the sunsets feel heavier than they ever did before. Every time the sun sets to dusk, I think of the questions I never got to ask you when you were still by my side. Of course, right after you leave for the sky, I realize I always saw myself in you, but I can't figure out why I never told you that. Now that the world goes on without you here, you've been living in my mind more than you had before.

I think of you in every sunset and moonrise, and while I drift into thoughts of you, the regrets get louder and louder. You live in my mind, but it is kind of saddening, a little comforting, and a pinch unbearable. I think about the sunsets you will miss. I think about never touching the soft wrinkles of your hand and I think about how I never told you certain things or asked you certain things because I thought you would be here longer. Most of all, though, I think about how my bottles of red nail polish by the windowsill seem fuller than ever before because I will never be able to paint your nails again.

To me, red nails are you. So I can't explain to everyone why, when I see my coworker's long red nails clicking away on a keyboard on a random Monday, I wince a little, and my eyes sting. I see you everywhere these days, but most of all I see you in me.

I don't like going downstairs into your room anymore because you aren't sitting on the edge of your bed putting on that overly scented powder that you always used to wear. When I do go to your room though, I flip through pictures of you from when you were my age. Why is it only now that I notice how your eyes are almond-shaped but big when you are happy, just like mine? Or how your top lip bends right when you smile in pictures?

I see the pot of eyeliner still atop your dresser, and I want to tell you that I still smudge my eyeliner out with my pointer finger the way you did it for me for the first time a decade ago. On the days I don't like my face as much, I remember that your features survived through generations with tenacity and my face is a little piece of you still here.

I used to love your room, especially years ago when I could run in here in the middle of the night after a nightmare and you would pat my back until I fell asleep. Now this room makes me feel empty, because it reminds me of how far away you are, and when you're far away, how am I supposed to run from my nightmares?

I want to tell you that every Friday afternoon I watch your favorite movies and try to laugh during the parts that you always laughed at since you will never watch a movie with me again. I want to tell you that I still like lettuce on my sandwiches, but not ketchup anymore like I used to. It's strange, though, because ever since you left, I have been taking the top slice off and putting ketchup on in a swirl before putting the top slice back on. It will never be as perfect as when you did it, no matter how hard I try. I want to tell you that I started going to that little park in the neighborhood again because I always want to remember the path that we walked on together—you with your red nails.

Every time the sun sets into dusk without you, I find it a little sad, a little comforting, and a pinch unbearable that we are moving through the days without you.

I just want you to know that I will paint my nails red and smudge my eyes with eyeliner until we can walk to the park together again.

jasmine air on the veranda

It is starting to feel like I always find myself in places I wish I never had to go to, and most of the time, it is usually arguing across from you. I am across from you often, trying to make you understand me and failing repeatedly.

Usually, I let the weather inside of me rise until my rage takes over and I am painfully warm to the touch. I wonder why I always end up across from you, with you always telling me how I should change. I get furious with you, wondering how you manage to always misunderstand me and how I cannot help but take it to heart. I know deep inside that the reason it hurts me so much is because I feel like you don't really know who I am, or maybe you do, but you don't like it. I wish you would just understand or at least try to understand the complicated weather inside of me, but whenever you hear about it, you just want to change it.

When the weather is too cold, we put a jacket on to keep warm, and when the weather is too warm, we take our layers off to keep cool. We always fight the weather, reversing it to keep comfortable. It feels better, but you never really know the weather that way, and you never actually feel it. I know this is what you do with me every time we argue because you would rather stay comfortable than feel my weather for what it is.

I wonder how it was so simple before when the love between us was not clouded with bitter misunderstandings and trauma that crept through generations. Sometimes when we argue, I look at you and wonder why we are always across from each other these days and never next to each other. I feel bad for me but also for you because I realize your misunderstanding is not new, it has been brewing for generations. Maybe you have been misunderstood, too, with someone always across from you, telling you how to change.

It doesn't happen often, but sometimes when we argue, I hear the weather inside of me go blank, and I just focus my eyes on yours. When I do, I go to this other place, one that I wish I could always go to in moments like this. I am not sure if I have ever been here, or if I will ever go, but I feel like it has always been ingrained in my mind.

In this place, you are sitting next to me, not across. We are sitting on our wooden swing, right outside our off-white house. It is just after morning, the beginning of a foggy afternoon. The sky is a light orange, and the silhouette of the trees surrounds us. I feel a slight breeze in my hair, and I see it in yours after you push the strands away from your face and tuck them behind your ear.

There is a slight scent of jasmine air on the veranda, maybe from the little jasmine petals you put in your grey-streaked hair. My legs are bent out to the left of me while I lay in your lap, looking up at the foggy sky. We both have slight goosebumps on our skin from feeling the cool wind, but we always wear matching nightgowns no matter what the weather is.

You are sitting across from the stone path that leads to our house, which is aligned with shrubs of jasmine and dark pink roses. Music is playing from inside our house that we can hear because we left the windows and door open, with the curtains blowing. In front of us is a table with two little teacups, the tea growing cold because we are busy talking.

We are talking next to each other, laughing about how we made the tea too strong again. We talk for hours about why we are here on earth, why we are here on the swing, and you put more jasmine petals in my hair until the moon forms itself in the sky, fuller than ever.

When we argue, I go back to the jasmine air on the veranda, partially because that is where we understand each other but mostly because that is where we feel the weather instead of trying to change it.

twenty-four flowers

Some afternoons are more unsettling than others, like today when I am bored and aimless. I am wandering the rooms of my house, purposefully trying to pretend it is all new to me to see what items I would still notice. I have been here for years, and sometimes I am afraid that I am so used to my space that I do not notice its charm anymore.

I brought in a brand-new bouquet today, made of twenty-four blush-colored flowers. I wander into the sunroom at the corner of my house, bouquet in hand. I look at all of the vases in the room, some clear, some that are colored glass. There are small ones and big ones, and they line the entire room while the sun bounces off of them and the afternoon light streams so delicately throughout the space.

Each vase has character and personality, none of them look alike. The only thing that all the vases have in common is that they are empty, completely void of a flower. When I think of this house as a new space that I am not used to, the emptiness of the vases is unsettling and dim, but deep inside I know why they are the way they are.

The most precious things I have ever owned are bouquets of flowers. I get a new bouquet every day from my garden. There are always twenty-four flowers for twenty-four hours. The flowers are all my time, and sometimes twenty-four flowers seem like a lot, but it is barely any flowers at all.

I remember a while ago before I started collecting empty vases, I found my bouquets easy to lose. I used to hold the stems loosely because no matter what I did, the flowers would inevitably escape me by the end of the day. The blooms are so beautiful, and even though they are precious to me, it used to be somewhat easy for me to share them.

I used to twirl them between my thumbs and give them to people—some who loved them and others who barely appreciated them. I never thought much of it, especially since the bouquets seemed infinite at first since I get a new one every day. At the end of the day, I felt wilted, and there were times when I did not even know where any of my twenty-four flowers went, so I promised to pay more attention to tomorrow's bouquet. When tomorrow came, I would forget all over again, and the stems would roll off of my hands without a vase to fall into.

There was an afternoon in particular when I remember exactly how I lost all my flowers of the day, and that was the day I finally learned to stop loosely twirling the blooms between my fingers. I had made three new friends around that time, and one day we planned to go on a walk to see the sunset over the hills.

I remember it was my first time having friends who wanted to experience the sun falling together, and I looked forward to it every afternoon until the day came. When the day finally came, I put on a pale blue dress and loosely held my flowers. I had planned to share my flowers with them after we watched the sunset together. I started walking towards the hill, feeling my excitement blend in with the afternoon air around me.

One of my friends showed up halfway, and I was surprised to see her. She tells me that one of the other friends is sick and that we will not be able to watch the sunset this afternoon after all. My face falls in disappointment as she tells me to walk back home. I gave her most of the flowers I was holding and told her that I felt sorry for our sick friend. I start to walk back, but I decide to watch the sunset anyway, even if it would be alone. I head for the hill again, walking all the way back. When I get to the hill, I sit on a patch of grass, realizing my last couple of flowers must have slipped through my fingers. I look down and see my pale blue dress on my knees and an empty stem across my legs. I look up to the sky to see the shades of violent orange and red in it like it was angry and resentful.

When I think about what might have upset the sky today, I hear laughter in the distance. I glance over my right shoulder and see my three friends. They look well, laughing and holding hands while they watch the sunset. It was then that I realized I had been giving my flowers to people who did not actually want to watch the sunset with me. It made my chest and stomach feel empty and void like something was wrong with me. That afternoon, when the tears on my face and the rays of the sun both went down, was when I decided that I would always hold onto my flowers.

That had been so long ago, and now I cannot even remember how it felt to not grip my flowers so tight that it physically ached. I still hand flowers out to people, but very carefully and delicately, because when I remember that angry sunset that happened decades ago, I feel like an empty vase myself.

I loosen the grip on the blush-colored bouquet that I am holding today and watch all twenty-four of them fall into a vase.

pumpkins in sepia

Between the books on my shelf, I have a little box wedged in the middle. It has a delicate little lock on it because I do not open the box too often. There have been a few afternoons that I have opened it up, though, and when I do, I take the delicate little key that I hide in my nightstand drawer and open the delicate little box. It is filled with photos and cassette tapes from my earliest days.

My parents had an extensive collection of moments from my childhood, some that were photos, and others that were messy little movies from when I was a baby or a young girl. I rarely find an afternoon to sit and watch the videos all the way through, but whenever I do watch them, I am always filled with this weird sensation where it feels like the memory I was watching back was just about to slip away from me but seeing it on a screen brought it back to me and renewed the memory in my head, at least for a couple more years.

The last afternoon I had gone through the memories with my parents was a few years ago, and I slipped the ones that made me feel extra nostalgic into my delicate little box. This afternoon, I felt like going through them again, and unlike most days, I had nothing else to do. I wanted to grasp all the details of every picture and try to put myself into a state of nostalgia.

I know what my story is right now and today, but sometimes I lose sight of what my story used to be, especially that long ago.

The first picture I picked up was me between both my parents on a cruise ship as they held me up in the air. I was smiling brightly, had melted ice cream dripping down the front of my shirt, and my hair tied in two little curly ponytails. I smile remembering how warm and carefree I must have felt when it was taken, but it is nowhere near as bright as my smile was in the picture.

I glance quickly at the background of the picture, noticing the decor on the ship that is probably considered vintage now. Even the sun looked warmer and sepia-toned. I look at how the jeans were baggier back then, the hair fluffier, and how the logos were much bigger on the clothes. I look at the background even closer, and I notice her.

Her, as in the woman in the background, even though I have not and will never meet her. I wonder what her name was or whether she was still alive. I wonder if she was always as happy as she looks in the background of my photo. I wonder what makes her tick, if she likes celery, and whether she's a morning person. I look at her again and think maybe she likes to collect coffee mugs. She probably likes to garden and then make a bouquet of her own flowers, enjoying how the stems feel being twirled around in her palms. She probably had a couple of kids and made them bouquets for their weddings. Now she is probably very old, drinking tea on a rocking chair in her living room that faces the sun. Her cupboards are probably still overflowing with coffee mugs, though, and I hope she closes her eyes a little every time she sits in her sunny rocking chair. I feel a heavy pang inside hoping that the story I made up was true, and hoping hard that she is alive and happy. I wonder if I am in the background of her photos, too. I put the picture back and picked up a cassette tape. My fingers collect a little dust, and I put it in the player.

A video starts playing of me dressed as a pumpkin on Halloween, running around a blue-green faded apartment complex, with my mother chasing me, laughing. There are scratches against the video, but it makes it feel even warmer. It abruptly cuts to me saying, "Trick or treat!" but not being able to properly pronounce it to one of our neighbors. He had white, fluffy hair, wrinkled skin, and a smile I remembered nearly twenty years later. He opened the door and filled my pink pumpkin basket to the top with those little caramel circle candies with twisted ties on either end. He told me about how pumpkins were special and how much he loved pumpkin pie.

I smile when I remember how special he made me feel and how I had a soft spot for pumpkins ever since. I wonder about him—how he probably was not around anymore and how I never knew his name. I wonder if those caramel candies were his favorite and how many pumpkin pies he had eaten in his life. He probably loved to bake but tried to take a bite of his desserts right when they came out of the oven and burnt his mouth a few times. He probably loved steaming hot espresso in the morning and sitting at the park to feed the birds. I hope he had pumpkin pie a few more times after I met him and that more people had rang his doorbell after I did. I wonder if there are pumpkins wherever he is, but I know for sure that there are. Most of all, though, I wonder if he had ever remembered me dressed like a cheery pumpkin every fall season because every time fall comes around and there are pumpkins everywhere, I remember him.

Closing the box for the afternoon, I think about whether

people notice me in the backgrounds of their memories—and wonder about the stories they make up for me.

liminal spaces

I have been in liminal spaces, but it was only recently that I started to feel like one. They are so strangely familiar and almost too real to the point where it feels chilling. They lay low, because they are nothing but the space in between. Liminal spaces are saddening to me because all they do is remind me of what they could have been if people had stayed in the picture.

I heard the mall from my childhood was close to closing down, and something led me all the way there this afternoon, even though I am far away from it now. I had to go see its emptiness because the only memories I have of it are full of life.

When I get there, it is familiar and unrecognizable at the same time. It is desolate and lonely, with the letters falling off the directories. This is probably the most nostalgic place I have left, but it is losing its charm between its liminal spaces. The lights of the store signs are still lit, but I guess they have been slowly fading during the past two decades. A couple of the stores are open—one or two employees aimlessly sitting inside. I wonder if they know what it used to be like here, when I was younger.

My favorite candy quarter machines are still there, collecting dust and looking dull. I look at it, trying to remember how bright the candy was to me as a child. Now it's barely saturated and looks tasteless like nobody has wanted candy for years.

The open space outside the stores is the most unsettling, with the fading patterned carpet and air that feels decades expired. I wonder where the magical air I had felt when I was twelve had gone, but it must be a world away. I glide my hand against a glass panel under the wall against the long-discontinued carousel. The dust attaches to the indents in my fingers as if it is begging me to hold on, and I think about how the architect must have felt when they put up these panels for the first time. I feel a pang thinking about how they were probably so hopeful in their creation—thinking of it as brand new and long-lasting. The carousel probably has not spun in a decade, and I momentarily feel grateful that I had spun on it back when it was a shiny red.

There is a stinging pain inside my chest as I think about all the candles that were blown out here during all the birthdays celebrated by children who are not children anymore. I walk for a little, making it through this expired air and past the barren stores. I come across an empty coffee bar counter. There's dust against the chairs and crumpled receipts marked with old dates. I see a few empty coffee cups that probably haven't met lips in the past year. I'm thinking of all the first dates that happened here or the old friends that ran into each other during Christmas shopping. The memories seem to be fading as I look around, my younger years feeling further and further away from me.

I feel for this mall, or the beach during the after-hours, or a field of wheat at night, or maybe a pretty parking garage after it's closed. They are beautiful, have a purpose, and most of all, they are visited by lots of people when they are open and bright. Sometimes when places get dim, people stop visiting because it no longer conveniences them. I'm not sure why people don't visit the beach during the after-hours, whether it's because they don't find it as beautiful anymore, or maybe it becomes harder to show up and see the ocean for its true colors.

Whatever it is, fewer people show up when things become unclear or harder to get to, and I guess it makes sense because the one time I went to a wheat field during the dark, I almost forgot how pretty it was during the daytime. I have to remind myself that the wheat fields had been the same color the whole time, the way my true colors are the same whether I feel bright or liminal.

I have phases, some more liminal than others, and I know people can tell. I am easier to visit on the beach during sunrise, but when my expired air and liminal spaces shine through, people stop visiting. I wish that when people found my liminal spaces, they could see me for what I really am, but I guess the expired air is all-consuming.

So when I closed the door behind me in my old mall that day, I made sure to hold on to its fading charm, even between its liminal spaces.

a lighter dance

It's loud and overcrowded with people, and there are lights of all kinds of colors flashing around the room. I had enough sips to feel lighter, but I can still think. I feel like I can let go a little looser than usual. I am dancing in this club tonight, my arms and feet moving with my friends around me and the music blaring throughout the walls. Being around this many people all at once with all the lights and noise is usually overstimulating and draining, like I'm losing connection with myself and can't think straight. That might be a part of the reason I had a few extra sips tonight.

I have my arms up, my feet moving, and feel my friend playfully hit her hip against mine. I feel the sobriety start to kick in a little, and I can hear my thoughts come back to me a little louder. My thoughts take me back to three heavy afternoons from when I was twelve years old, in the passenger seat of the family van.

My mom was driving me to the first of three dance classes, even though it was the last thing I had ever wanted to do. I knew I would not enjoy it because I was not naturally rhythmic with my body, but my mom was excited. She was telling me about the outfits she would help me choose and how she would be so proud when she could watch the performance with me onstage for the first time. I agreed to go because the excitement in her voice was pure and I was convinced I needed to give it a try.

During the first class, my teacher pulled me aside to tell me that I was too rigid and too poised. She said I would have to work harder than the rest of the girls to get up to speed for the performance. My mom was excited to see me after, and I had to pretend like I did well when, in reality, I had failed. I failed in the beginning, I failed in the middle, and I failed in the end, too.

I practiced at home a couple of times before the next class, and I thought I had done a lot better because the teacher did not pull me aside this time. I felt like I was in sync, and my body moved in a more fluid way. I told my mom I improved after class and felt like I belonged as much as the other girls.

The third class came around, and I felt like my practice was paying off. I had started to remember the steps better, and I had been practicing at home. My mom came a few minutes earlier to pick me up, and she looked through the clear glass to watch me. She was happy to see me doing something out of my comfort zone, and I made sure to smile when she was here even though I did not feel passionate or happy about doing this. Class finished, and my dance teacher walked out, but I stayed behind for a minute to drink from my water bottle before I went.

When I left, I saw my teacher talking to my mom, so I stepped back so I could hear what they were saying. My mom looked disappointed as my teacher told her I was rigid and unteachable. She told my mom that she had to take me off of the team because I was going to hurt their performance. I don't know what I felt when I first heard that, but when I followed my mom into the car, I knew she was finding a way to tell me that would not pull me down. Her looking me in the eyes and struggling to tell me stung in a way that left a mark.

My mom told me reluctantly that the performance got canceled and it had nothing to do with me. Remembering how excited my mom was before the first class showered me with guilt, and I was frighteningly frustrated at how incapable I was. The performance she had wanted to see me in would go on without me. I brought the other girls down, and my teacher was scared I would hurt their performance. I did not belong here after all. It left a scar on me that would periodically show up, even though it is ten years later.

I still have my arms up and my feet moving, and I know I'm a little more rigid than the rest of the crowd here.

It just feels lighter than it did during those three afternoons.

strawberry sundays

You were eating strawberry ice cream on a hot Sunday after-noon in July, and it was my first memory of our strawberry Sundays. I remember turning and looking up at you, blissfully eating the light, pink-tinted ice cream out of a waffle cone. You close your eyes when the cold reaches your forehead. Just one scoop for you because it melts faster than you can eat it. You hold it in front of me with a smile, and I take my first bite of strawberry ice cream, getting it all over my nose. It is your favorite flavor, and now it is mine, too.

Since then, we started eating ice cream every Sunday after-noon, and it was just the two of us eating the strawberry carton. Nobody in our house liked it as much as the two of us. This one time, I remember, we went to a little ice cream shop, and we got it in a bowl. Two spoons in the cup, just two scoops, one for each of us. We tap our spoons together and smile because it is the both of us, always.

We got along when I was younger—whe n I still fit into the small shadow you left behind. I had always done what you told me, thinking it would always lead me the right way. As years and many strawberr y Sundays passed, I outgrew your shadow and started adding my flawed touch to everything I did instead of always doing what I was told. Even though it was my flawed touch, I liked that it was mine instead of anyone else's, but I think you preferred me when I fit into the small shadow you left behind.

The day I broke out of your shadow was when we went on a walk one Sunday afternoon, and it was my first time wearing flip-flops. They were too big, so you told me not to run wearing them, but I wanted to see what would happen if I did not listen to you just this one time. I ran in them, and afterward, you did what seemed unimaginable at the time. You did not speak to me for three days, and it did not seem like it stung that hard for you.

Three long, excruciatingly hot summer afternoons without you because I made a mistake. On the third afternoon, I walked by the dining table and saw you there with one scoop of strawberry ice cream in front of you. I thought strawberry Sundays were ours, but I guess it was yours all along.

After that afternoon, there were a couple of other times I saw you eating it alone, and even though I wanted to grab my spoon and put it in your cup, I was scared you did not have room for me across from you anymore. It got a little harder to talk to you, and even though I wanted to, I wondered if it was easier for you if I did not. The few times that you did sit across from me, there were two spoons, two scoops, and one cup. When you had strawberry Sundays without me, though, it would make me wonder if you missed me like I always did when I saw you alone or if you enjoyed the peace. I thought you might have just been mad, and I thought you liked strawberry Sundays better with me.

There was a time when I tried to put my spoon in your cup to see if I just had to make room for myself across from you since you did not want to make that room for me. You get up, already being finished, and don't even notice me sitting across from you. I slowly and painfully realized over the years that you wanted your own strawberry Sundays, at least on most afternoons.

I eventually learned to have my own strawberry Sundays— just one scoop because it melts faster than I can eat it. I learned to eat it alone and not look across from me to check for you. After several summers, it started to taste sweet again, even when you ate yours alone without joining me. I am fine with eating strawberry ice cream alone now, but so many summers have passed since we ate our two scoops together. Sometimes, I even wanted to try eating it with you again, even though I was scared you did not want to share your strawberry Sundays with me anymore and angry that you could go without talking to me, but I had trouble without you.

One day, when I wanted someone, anyone across from me, I inhaled and put one scoop in one cup, sticking my spoon on the side. I hand it to you, but you don't say anything. You take it and close your eyes when the cold reaches your forehead, just like you did on our very first strawberry Sunday. Even though you like the ice cream, it did not feel like there was room for my spoon in your cup anymore.

The memories ache, but I love my strawberry Sundays alone now. This afternoon, years later, I am here in this diner and have strawberry ice cream in front of me. Part of me wishes you were across from me, but it is easier for me to eat it alone than ever before and every bite is sweet.

The cold reaches my head, and I look forward to all of my upcoming, easier strawberry Sundays—whether they are alone or with you.

first flicker

When I moved into my apartment a year ago, I needed a table for when I worked or ate. It was the first piece of furniture I bought after my bed, and it felt like a big moment. Creating my own safe space was something I had been looking forward to for years, and this table would collect so many memories.

I went to the furniture store, and I browsed around for hours for my sacred safe space. I finally found a round table with three chairs around it. It's a light wood, textured, but not so much that it would be hard to clean. The chairs were inviting, like they were begging you to pause and lean back a little. It fit the rest of my space perfectly and was the only furniture in my apartment that welcomed someone to sit with me.

I put a tall, cream-colored candle on top that I light for a few minutes every day while I eat or read. There was a chair facing the television and a chair to its left and right in a triangle shape around my table. The left chair was mine—I never sat in the other ones. I was right about how many memories this table would collect.

Every morning, I'd take my first sips of the day there, and in the afternoon, I would read or type on its surface. There were a few times when I fell asleep there or had my knees up on the chair crying on my harder nights. The candle melted at an angle, getting shorter every day. A year later, the candle is half its size, and I still only use the left chair.

Last night, I invited him over, even though we were in a bad place. I thought I could tell him about the way he made me feel because everyone always says communication can solve anything. He agreed, and when he came, he sat in the left chair, the one that was mine.

I'm sitting on my couch that I bought after my table so that I can see him in full light. I'm telling him how upset I felt after certain things he said and how many tears my table had to hold for me these past few months.

He doesn't listen, though—he says it is my fault for feeling that way. He raises his voice a little, and it's the first time. He throws his hands up in the air out of frustration, and my candle falls to the floor.

All I can remember now is the image of him sitting in my sacred space and yelling at me. It made me afraid of my own chair, my own space. Now when I take my first sips in my chair, I feel uneasy. I quit sitting at my table and started sitting on my couch instead.

Whenever I do, I glance over at my table, and the image of him being upset with me from my chair crosses my mind every few minutes. I decided one afternoon that I didn't need all three chairs. The trash area is a few floors under my floor, so I take my left chair and push it out the window. I watch it shatter when it hits the ground.

I push the two chairs I have left to be across from each other. Then I light a new cream-colored candle and watch it flicker for the first time. I sit in the chair that used to face right, and it feels a little safer.

The chair across from me—it's open.

alps

Today is three hundred and ten days since you and I went to the mountains together. Our four feet were here then, but today it is just my two.

When we went last time, my two feet were behind yours. I remember looking up and seeing the veins in your arms pulling me forward. I remember seeing you stretching your arms against the autumn skyline and realizing how tall your silhouette was. I remember you saying we were crazy for coming out here in the fall, but you did because it was my favorite season, and then I wrapped a blanket around the both of us, and we waited for the world around us to dim and the stars to start shining through. I remember waiting for your earthy voice and letting it guide me. I remember burying my head in your chest, barely hearing the wind around us.

Today, it's just my two feet. I wonder where you are, but I only let that thought last half a second. I took the same route that you taught me, but for some reason, things are different today. It is harder to pull myself forward, but when I do, there's this breeze of cold air against my skin. I can pause and sit down against the earth. I notice this thick mist around me, and how the sky is beautifully furious shades of ember and mulberry. It reminds me of why I anxiously wait for this season every year.

I came alone, and when I was standing with these mountains in front of me, these valleys beside me, and the sky behind me, I felt small.

Small in a colossal way, as if I could trust fall into these shades of ember and nothing would ever happen to me. I would be protected no matter what. The sense of protection you experience after surviving the worst.

When I get cold, I just lay down against this earth, and look up at the silver specks in the sky. No matter how far I stretch my arms on the ground, there is infinite space to grow. I think it's because I'm not with you tonight.

Your voice is melting away, and I'm hearing the earth again.

our song on the jukebox

I don't know at what age I fell off track with what day it was, but I think it's Tuesday right before sunset. The day of the week, like many other things that used to concern me, does not matter much anymore. It is a cool summer night, and we ventured a bit further than usual— all the way to the diner where both of us met fifty years ago.

We are so calm these days, and I am glad because it took nearly all my life to achieve being this stress-free. During the afternoons, we usually just sit on our old wicker chairs, but I think I was craving the restlessness of my youth today. We decided to go back fifty years, so I decided to surprise him by wearing the outfit we met in, that I secretly kept in a box for the past five decades. It is an overall dress, with a white T-shirt under it that has red hearts all over it. I guess he had the same idea, because he showed up wearing that red and black varsity jacket I never stopped loving on him.

When we enter the diner hand-in-hand, I hear that chime that takes me back to when I used to run in here through my teenage years. There are straw containers filled with those same red and white paper straws and shiny, red cherries atop all of the sundaes people are eating. He lets go of my hand and walks up to the counter to ask for help getting the jukebox running again.

I just sit in a booth while I wait, taking in the new changes here that must have happened while my skin started to wrinkle and my hair started to grey. The jukebox is in its same spot, all these years later, but now it is just decor.

It was that one song on the jukebox, where he held out his hand and spun me around, and my smile could not have been bigger. I never could remember the name of the song, but he knew it and never told me. We would just dance to it whenever we came here all those years ago, sipping on milkshakes in between.

He had always been more extroverted than me, especially because I am not one to draw attention to myself in public. He is loud and bright, though, like always. Year after year, he never fails to get the room to fall in love with him—and fall in love with themselves. I was never shocked, except once when I was twenty, that I had fallen for him on the night that we first spoke.

The jukebox begins to stream music, a little muffled but still with its charm. The sound of it reminds me of coming here after school, of all the autumns and springs I spent in my twenties, and of meeting him. I smile when I see his smile at the music starting and watch him spin around. Unsurprisingly, everyone in the room looks up from their sundaes and their worries to admire the bounce in his steps as he dances to the tune.

They see an old man wearing a varsity jacket, but I see the twenty-something who held his hand out to me. I don't dance anymore, but I love watching him because it reminds me of who we still are, and no matter how long we have lived, we always need a reminder of who we are. I think of the night we ran out of here to take our first shots together, the night we pierced each other's ears for fun, and most of all I remember what it feels like to be restlessly in love.

I am lost in thought and a soft smile as I see him laughing and dancing. The song slowly transitions into that one song that used to play on the jukebox—our song on the jukebox.

I feel a flurry in my heart, the same I felt when I met him. He dances over to the booth that I am sitting in and holds his hand out again. I hesitate, but since it's our song on the jukebox, I roll my eyes at him and put my hand in his.

My overalls flounce as he spins me, and I realize how restlessly in love I am.

dusk to
afterhours

my teaspoon on your plate

The breeze outside reminds me of 1997, and I am not going to let it go just yet. I gave up blow-drying my hair so now the top of it is dry and refined, and the ends are unruly and curly. I look in the mirror, outlining my lips with a shade of dark brown. Part of me likes the uneasy excitement buzzing inside of me and part of me would do anything to make it go away. I put on a slip dress, a shade of maroon that brings out the brown in my eyes. I lock the door to my room and start playing bossa nova music, songs that amplify the feeling of not being able to get that new person out of your head. I spin around the empty spaces in my room because I have extra time and I need to do something with this foreign buzz I am feeling. My hair is even more tousled now, pouring over my shoulders.

I eventually make it to the restaurant with him, the buzz turning into nervous flurries that make me laugh more than usual. We're walking into the dimly lit restaurant hand-in-hand, and he's looking straight ahead while I look up at his shoulder. I look away subtly when I know I feel his eyes move towards me. The tables are dark brown, with red upholstery on the chairs. The lighting is dim enough so it is not harsh on your eyes but just lit enough that you can see who you are here with. There are a few hours of our laughter blending into the jazzy bossa nova music in the background and my heels hitting against each other out of nervousness. I think I already know how I feel about him, but I just want one more sign to be sure because it would be hard if I was wrong. I'm not listening to his words about the niceties around us, but I'm taking in the way he moves his hands while he speaks.

Our hands accidentally touch, and even though we have gone out a couple of times before, it still makes me nervous. The waiter is standing behind him, at a distance only in my view, and he catches my eyes and smiles in support. The waiter dances to the jazz that surrounds us and comes to our table. "Anything else?" he offers.

I order a tea to calm myself down. The waiter places it down right in front of me, and we keep talking while I sip on it slowly. I pick up a teaspoon to stir in a little sugar while I listen to him talk about his affinity for lighthouses. He tells me he loves how the ocean never ends, and how lighthouses are the only way to navigate the never-ending.

I am done stirring in the sugar and pick up the teaspoon, holding the teacup with my other hand. The waiter had forgotten the saucer under my teacup and I did not want to stain the cream porcelains of the table. While I am telling him about how I am attached to lighthouses too, his eyes drop to my hand holding the teaspoon. He pushes a little plate from his side to mine until it is directly under my hand holding the spoon. He did it without looking down once or missing a single word that I said. He was nodding and giving me his gentle smiles, the kind that makes his eyes bend, and his dimples shine, all while I let the spoon fall onto the plate he pushed under it. I think this was the last thing I needed to not be afraid anymore that I was wrong about this one. We get up to leave and the waiter comes back to our spot. He shows me the saucer he had purposely left in his pocket.

"You're welcome," he says with a wink.

moscow mule

I was sitting at a table with three friends tonight in this restaurant in a city more than a few states away from home. I was feeling okay, maybe just a little insecure about how my hair or lips looked because this city seemed to only host the drop-dead gorgeous. There were three clear glasses of wine on this glass tabletop, with the neon blue sign in the reflection. The fourth was a shorter copper cup that hosted a Moscow mule, and it's the one I picked up and sipped from between taking photos of my beautiful friends and the ambiance that surrounded us. I usually love capturing the moment, especially in a place as beautiful as this one.

When it was my turn to pose alongside two of my friends, with the third friend taking the picture, I guess my insecurity shone through. It was something between my hair being a little out of place tonight or me remembering how I felt being photographed when I was six.

When I was six, my photographer told me my smile looked stiff as he moved from staring through the lens, back at me, to looking at what he could fix in my expression. I smiled at the camera, trying to stop my mind from sabotaging yet another photo. Right when I remembered how that photographer eventually led me to practice my smile before every photoshoot

I ever had, the friend who was taking the picture yet again told me that my smile looked posed. I got a little upset inside because I hate standing out, especially as the one who still hasn't figured out her smile at twenty-two.

I think this finally broke my fear of being the one with a flair for the dramatics, and I headed to the bathroom without telling any of them. I looked at myself in the mirror, wet the one curl that I was worried about, and watched it bounce back. I took out my lipstick bullet, tapping it in impatience and anger, and dabbed it upon my lips. After taking in my own reflection, I took a few pictures, away from the night's company, smiling or not smiling in the way that I prefer now that I was in my own solitude.

I came back, not completely sure of myself, but better than before, and sat down. My friend encouraged me to retake the picture, and I tried to smile again, knowing it was far from genuine. I heard my friends lightly chuckle and ask me if it would kill me to just smile for real. The need to repress my annoyance and depth of insecurity suddenly evaporated from my mind. I told them my smile was ingenuine, as they mercilessly suggested because maybe I just was not having an amazing time. I told them I didn't feel like remembering this moment anymore and was not feeling like taking any more pictures.

Later that night, we all found ourselves waiting for a taxi. We were standing together, and in front of us was a tall, old man hailing a taxi who bore no smile. He had deeply sunken eyes and delicate wrinkles on his skin. I caught the man looking at me for longer than a few seconds, so I smiled at him genuinely because I felt much better than before.

He took his hat down and proceeded to tell me that I had a

beautiful smile, one that reminded him of his daughter who he missed very much.

seasons at sunset

Tonight, while the moon was rising, I started to wonder if the seasons would still change if I stopped paying attention. Even though I have experienced many of each of the four seasons, sometimes I forget what they look like. I have too many moments when I can't quiet my mind, and it wanders so much that I don't notice the seasons anymore.

I recently was given a car, one that goes to all four seasons in one trip. The car has been there for a few weeks, but my mind has been extra noisy lately, so I waited to go on a trip until it quieted down. I realized that waiting for my mind to calm down to a quieter state made the seasons shorter because they ended as soon as I was ready. It was sunset now, and I noticed the car door was left open, the setting sun shining inside the interior. I decided to stop waiting, and sat behind the wheel, even though my mind was not quiet.

I strap myself into the car and turn on my favorite instrumen-tals, noticing the piano reverberate throughout my car. I start it up and drive away from my house. I have been driving on back roads for a couple of minutes now, and I end up driving to a forest I have never seen before.

It is winter here, and there are evergreens lining my entire view, my eyes being the only limit. The branches are covered in snow, clinging onto the dark green needles. The sunset is shades of soothing plum and scarlet, with the red sun shining against it. A few deer are around, their footprints being the only mark imprinting the pure white. Even though the trees are so tall, they still found room for the sun to shine its last light of the day through them. I want to add my imprint in the snow, too, but on the inside, I feel like it doesn't belong there. I keep driving through the strangely beautiful winter. I drive past miles of evergreens and notice the snow gradually melting as I go through them.

I eventually notice the showers of rain, and light colors coming back after the winter. I am in spring now, and the flowers are standing up a little straighter than usual. The sun is setting, and the sky is grey and hazy above the light orange sunset. There are cherry blossoms all around and patches of flowers all over the ground. I drive further, past the forest, and I come to a large grass patch. I see picnic blankets spread all throughout, ones that are different shades of pastel colors with woven baskets in between. Some of them have sleeping bunnies on them, one sleeping peacefully atop a pile of flowers. That bunny makes me feel warm inside—I am happy he was able to find rest in our world where rest has become rare. There are no people around, but it is clear there were. My mind feels quieter, the only noise being the rustle in the breeze and the birds drifting off. The clouds are so low in the sky that it feels like I could jump through them, but I decide to keep driving. The heavy showers gradually turn lighter and lighter until the rain completely disappears.

I see a beach sunset in the left window of my car, and I see stretches of sand and water. I am in summer now, the cerulean waters sparkling from the last reflections of the yellow-orange sun. The sky is dark blue at the top but blends into an angry orange at the bottom against the ocean. I drive slower and turn the music down so that I can hear the waves hitting the sand. Each wave crashing makes me feel sad inside for some reason, reminding me of all the things I wanted to do but never did. I watch the waves for a while until tears well up inside my eyes. I notice the seagulls flying above my car and cattails dancing proudly against the shore. I want to remember this summer forever, so I drive slowly. I drive slowly until I remember absolutely everything I never did and every moment I never had.

Eventually, I made it into a forest again, but this one was all calming shades of brown and red because I made it to fall. The sunset is mostly orange, but there is a blended stripe of a light lilac lost somewhere in there. There are tall trees everywhere, their leaves slowly separating from them. Even though it seems like it should be sad that the leaves leave the tree, they fall humbly and effortlessly onto the ground as if they know they will join the trees again soon. Everything around me is orange, brown, and gold, and there are piles of leaves everywhere. As I drive through them, they blow up into the air and fall upon my windows to remind me that fall is when nature changes. I drive slower than ever, trying to understand how the trees still stand strongly even when all of their leaves have abandoned them. While the sun sets, its rays shine all around it, illuminating the different shades of fall. I can see mountains in the far distance, their surfaces faintly brown.

A variety of leaves cover my window and I eventually reach a wooden bridge in the middle of the forest. I come out of the car for the first time during this drive, sitting on the bridge with my knees touching my chin. I hear animals in the distance, their voices of mahogany melting into the wind. I feel absolutely nothing inside, and my mind is mostly quiet. I close my eyes, letting my hair blow in the anxious fall wind. I pick up a red leaf and twirl its stem between my fingers. I fall asleep on the bridge for hours, and when I wake up, I am covered in a pile of leaves. I know it is still fall, though, because the leaves are still falling, the wind is still blowing, and the sky is still darkening.

I look up one last time at how quickly and effortlessly nature could change during one drive and wonder why I am different.

party of embers

My nighttime dreams feel like places that I have never been to before with people that I know but haven't met. They feel like events that I have gone to, but I have never left my trace behind there for anyone to find. It feels hazy like I can't remember whether it really happened or if it really affected me. Sometimes I try to remember it and put it together, but the more that I wake up, the more that I can't feel whole. I used to get upset, but now I trust that the important ones will come back to me.

Maybe the ones that happen over and over again, the same event that I keep getting invited back to, the same place that I'm somewhat familiar with, are the ones that I should remember. Sometimes, when I am running a fever, I fall asleep and go to this one place that is so familiar that I cannot believe that I have not been there before.

I go to a room that stretches horizontally both ways pretty far, and I always start in the middle, where I can turn and look to the left, right, and then in a circle. I can try to see both ends of the room that way. The room has lighting that reminds me of liquid gold in its hue. There are small, high tables that would seat two or three people, but no chairs. I think this is because you are meant to lean on the table while you stand up to talk to the others around it. Everything in the room looks like a sunset because it is all shades of ember. No matter how many times I rotate around, I cannot see anything that is not a shade of golden yellow or a warm orange.

The background is so serene, that I almost always forget the unsettlement that follows without fail. In this room of ember, there are people at every corner and in between. People around me, behind me, and leaning on those high tables to talk to each other. Everyone is holding something orange and sparkly in their drinking glasses, and the tablecloth has golden trim. I can hear them chatting around me, clinking their glasses against each other, and everyone seems happy. All the different conversations sounded like they were full of heart. I focus on all the overlapping talk around me at this party to see if I can pick up anything familiar.

I stop looking around this party and pause to listen since everyone at this party is speaking languages that seem close to mine. I begin to get nervous because the language sounds so familiar and safe, but I cannot make out a single word. It is like I was supposed to understand, but everything is just slightly thrown off, and there is no one here to talk to or understand me. It is a little scary that I do not understand what anyone around me is saying like I am foreign in my own head. It is horrific when I realize that no one can understand me either.

There are so many people around me, but I just cannot communicate with them. I try to say something, but I cannot produce any sound no matter how hard I try. It is not that I am not speaking, it is that it is too hard to hear me. No matter how loud I scream or clutch my throat, it sounds like a whisper. Over and over and over and over and over again. Until I am right back to where I was earlier.

Usually, when I go somewhere new, I try to find the exit right away. Not because I want to leave, but in case I need to later. For some reason at this party of embers, I held off on trying to find the exits right away. I had an instinctual feeling that it would be hard, and since the golden hues made me feel warm, I did not think I would want to leave. Now that I cannot find anyone to speak or listen to, I need to find the exit.

I start from the middle and walk to the left. If there is no exit on the left, I plan to come back to the middle and walk to the right. I run through, noticing that every table has people at it and the tables went all the way to the left. I notice the tables are perfectly aligned, completely identical. The left side feels like it has no end, so I keep going and going.

The exit seems far away, and the voices become louder. I run back to the middle where I started and start heading right. It feels like I have been on the right side for hours, and it still seems endless. Everyone continues to clink their glasses and speak in a way I can't understand. No one pauses to listen to me—in fact, I must not be made of ember because they don't even notice me here. I want to leave this party of embers, a party where there is no room for me. I don't even know what direction I am in anymore, but I need to find safety, so I keep going and going.

I never can find the exit, though, and the chatter never stops. I keep running until I end up where I am now.

half glass of bubbly

I am walking the city streets a little after midnight, alone, with mascara flaked underneath my eyes and my bangs peeking out from my loosely tied ponytail. I had a couple of drinks earlier, but it was enough for me to feel just the right amount of carefree. I had fallen asleep on my bed right away but kept waking up every few minutes like I always do when I am hungover.

This time, though, I just got up and decided to find something to eat downtown, but truthfully, I also just wanted to get outside and experience the air of the after-hours for a little. My throat is dry, and my head is beating. I am a little hungry, but mostly I am restless and want to ignore the relaxation my body is asking for. I trust that after I stroll a few more blocks, I will finally stumble upon a place that is open during these odd hours, and maybe I can sit for a little and create life stories in my head for the others at the place while I drink the cup of decaf that I desperately need right now.

I feel a little empty-headed, in a good way, and also aimless, like my hair that is blowing in the cold air every which way. It was only a couple blocks of walking before I got to this quaint, almost hidden spot called Gold Bar that I hadn't noticed before. The tiny door has a little pane over it, and everything is shades of the same rich, golden brown. It seems inviting enough, especially with the red "24/7" neon sign out front being the only non-neutral color. I walk in through the door, automatically comforted by the sudden warmth and the windiness fading away. It is dimly lit inside, with most of the light being from warm, white candles of varying sizes that were placed all around the restaurant. My favorite part is the large row of photos of what Gold Bar used to look like when it opened decades ago.

There are a few people around, and most of them have someone sitting across from them with drinks and plates between them. I usually love sitting in the corner of all my favorite places and prefer making up stories for others around me instead of getting to know what their actual stories are. I am not sure what it is about tonight, but when I see the warmth of the people here and the candles in between them, I have a quick fleeting pang in my mind where I suppose it would have been nice to sit across from a friend during this restless night.

There are a few people ahead of me and I am not sure what I want to order yet, so I look around to see what everyone else has in front of them. My eyes take a momentary pause when I see a woman my age, with highlights in her long hair, and dark eyeshadow around her light brown eyes. She has half a glass of bubbles to the left of her and a basket of fries to her right. She is the only one here who does not have company this late at night, but she does have a little sketchbook that she is bent towards and engulfed in, the same way I am with my own art.

She has a few colored pencils in front of her and is furiously sketching in her book, her eyes focused on the page. I try to take a subtle glance at her work, but no matter how hard I try, her highlighted hair completely covers it. Missing my friends, I push my dark bangs back and walk towards her table.

"Those fries look good—I can't choose between those or the

apple pie," I say. I smile at her and notice her nails are painted the same shade of crimson that mine are. She smiles back, telling me that the right answer is always both and to sit with her so we can share. I am surprised at how warm she is and quickly contemplate what could go wrong with sitting across from a stranger this late at night. I want to know her and her art though, so I smile back.

I order my decaf and apple pie and then point to her to show the waiter where I am going to sit. I sit across from her and ask her about her day. She tells me she is new to the city and has only been here a week, and she shows me her sketchbook. She flips through it excitedly, like she has been waiting for this moment.

Her little book is filled with sketches of people that she met here, the buildings that she saw here, and even loaves of bread that she ate here. The sketches are real and raw. They remind me of the city sights I do not notice anymore, since I have been here for years. She keeps the last page covered, though, the one I tried to look at earlier. I cannot believe she is not here with her friends because she just has such a lively, bouncy energy about her that is so genuine.

A few minutes pass by, and the waiter gives me a tall, black mug and places a slice of pie between us. He confirms the mug is filled with hot decaf, and it allows me to feel at ease since he remembered to make it decaf. I put a little cream in the mug, and the woman chuckles. I ask her why, and she tells me she did not know anyone actually liked decaf, and I start laughing, too. I told her that this was the only thing that could ease my hangover, but caffeine would make me anxious. I comment on her half-glass of bubbly, asking if she is always this peppy or if it was the bubbles talking.

She laughs and tells me it hardly has an effect on her. I can tell the midnight skies are getting deeper and deeper as the after-hours pass because the candles in the Gold Bar are glowing brighter than before. The pie plate turns empty with two spoons laid on top of it and my mug of decaf disappears, my lipstick staining it.

I tell her about how I arranged my first bouquet of flowers this weekend, and she shows me a photo of her first attempt at crocheting. The skies are now getting lighter through the windows, and the candles are barely needed anymore. We talk about our favorite pies, our most gut-wrenching heartbreaks, and how lost we feel in our own minds.

I never got her name, but I did not think I needed to. She knows me now the way she would have if we had been friends for years—my highs, my lows, and my love for decaf. It already feels complete, and now I feel more complete. When we hug goodbye, it feels like a memory that happened long ago.

Not in a fleeting, insignificant way, but like something I am going to remember tomorrow, the week after that, and forever—especially when I see a glass of bubbly.

dark eyes and decaf

I have been going around my new city, finding spots that feel warm. I have one last page of my sketchbook left, and I am searching for the right picture to draw. It was my first time at this new spot called Gold Bar, but it felt familiar like I had been coming here for years.

I have been here since dusk and haven't left the same table, but I did have a couple of glasses of bubbly, and now one halfway finished is sitting next to me. I think the Gold Bar has always been 24/7, and I can see in the large, vintage photos hanging on the wall how the place progressed over the years.

I love how dim it is here and how the golden hues of all the candles fall upon my sketches. As warm as I feel, I wish I could meet a new friend—it does not have to be a forever person, but maybe someone to share a few stories with or show my sketches to. Maybe it is because no one is here alone, and I am surrounded by people immersed in conversation. I am here with just my art—which had always been my favorite company, but I kind of want to show people my sketches of the city because I am proud of them.

I have a basket of fries to the side of me and wish I had gone with something sweet instead, but I try to look around again to find something to sketch. I hear the door chime ring as the door closes, and a woman my age walks in, her dark bangs affected by the wind. I notice that her nails are the exact shade of crimson that mine are painted, and I am glad I have a crimson pencil.

I see her looking around, maybe taking in the ambiance or looking for order inspiration, and she walks towards me. She tells me my fries look good and she can't choose between sweet or salty. I look up at her and smile. "The right answer is always both. Do you want to sit here? We could share," I hear myself say. I realize that may have been desperate on my end, and almost regret saying it, but she returns a smile under her dark but bright eyes.

She orders a decaf coffee and a slice of pie, pointing towards me when the waiter asks her where she would like to sit. She asks me about my day, so I tell her about my new findings in the city and ask her what her favorites are. I show her my sketch of the buildings I can see out of my window, a few people I met on the train, and even a loaf of bread I bought at the bakery in the corner. Her dark eyes are scanning the sketches, and I feel comforted because no one but my sister had ever been so curious about the sketches I draw for fun. She points out the details, like how some of the people I drew weren't smiling, or how the building windows faintly had the reflections of people inside them. Her genuine curiosity about it is warm and real. I can tell right away that she makes art herself.

The waiter places her black mug of decaf in the middle, and she lifts a spoon to add cream to it. I chuckle and tell her that she is the first person I have ever met to purposefully order decaf, and she tells me how much she loves it and needs it to cure her current hangover. She makes fun of me for actually liking champagne when I tell her that it does not really have much of an effect on me. She laughs while she tells me about how her head was beating from just a couple of drinks she had before.

I have not looked at my watch in a while, but I am sure it is past midnight. The pie had slowly disappeared, our two spoons now resting on the plate. I smile when I look at it because I did not think I would have found the company I needed tonight.

She asks about my favorite activities, and I show her the flawed bag I made crocheting for the first time. She says it is full of love and she wants one, too. "I made my first bouquet of flowers with a few different colors of peonies and baby's breath in between," she says. We talk about our most recent heartbreaks and agree that being alone and finding solace in feminine friendships are healing us little by little. I cannot imagine someone as put together as her feeling out of sorts in any way, but she tells me how confused she has been feeling in her own mind lately, just like me. It is the first time I've realized that other people feel like leaving their minds for a little while, too—or wish they had a map to get around it.

My watch buzzes to remind me to wake up, and I notice it is completely light outside now and I already am more awake than I have felt for a long time. I never got her name, but even when we hug goodbye, I do not think it is anywhere as important as the memory we just made in the past few hours. Most important of all, I know now why decaf coffee exists, and it makes me feel warm inside.

As she leaves, I decide to stay and finish my final sketch. My night and now the day has taken a strangely special and valuable turn, and I can tell I made the rare type of memory where, every few years, I will think of tonight and smile. The story behind her dark eyes and decaf can be a little part of my own story.

I smile when the last burning candle glows against my sketch of a black mug of decaf, with crimson nails holding it and a lipstick stain against it.

shell of petals

It was one night that he sympathetically called me an innocent flower, and it made me wonder whether people like flowers as anything but decoration nowadays. I was blindly mesmerized by him and embarrassed that he, and probably others, saw me as nothing but a shell of petals. Even though he made me doubt myself in a way that my stomach would churn inside, deep down I knew that even though flowers are mistaken for just decoration, they are often a gift for others if the receiver recognizes their beauty.

Flowers seem to flourish when they trust in their own story. Even though I have been sure of this for a long time, it still hurts when the objects of your affection don't recognize the bouquet of strong petals in front of them. It sent me into a spiral because I wish they viewed me the way I viewed me, instead of wilted empty petals.

In need of some watering, I called my friend over to my place because of the feeling of being alienated by yet another person—when all I wanted was to be recognized, hurt infinitely. She told me she would come by later that night and let me wallow in this heartbreak with someone by my side. I needed my friend that night because she understood my heart of hearts. She understood that I did not want to talk but just needed to lay low with company.

By the time she drove through the dark rainfall, it was past eleven at night. She found me clutching my knees to my chest on my bed, my curls pulled back and my eyes scarring from crying the past few hours. She asked me if I wanted to go to bed, but I told her that even though I was not rested, I didn't want to rest. I needed to leave the bed I'd been clutching to for the past few days.

I told her to take me on a drive, even though I hadn't slept or eaten. We ran through the rain, my blanket around the both of us. There was a little space between our backs and the blanket where the wind was pushing through. We climbed into her car, and she turned the heater on. We were silent, but it was comforting and warm, just the rain pouring onto the window so hard that we had to drive slower and push ourselves closer to the window to see.

We drove a mile or so, and she pulled into a drive-thru to get me a strawberry milkshake because she remembered that I lose my appetite when I get like this, but sipping through a straw is a lot easier. She handed it to me and drove back onto the road. I took the first sip and put the straw under her mouth while she turned the wheel. I thought about how lucky I am that love comes through in friendships, too, because sometimes when we chase it only where our stomach churns, we forget.

I hadn't cried since we came out of my apartment, and stopping made me feel how tired I was through my eyes and bones. The truth was that I try to sleep less when I'm upset because when I'm stressed, the nightmares are usually so much worse. I didn't want to be upset during both my waking life and my subconscious one, but I could feel the wave of sleepiness overtake me.

My eyes half open, I heard my friend humming delicately, the rain pattering hard against the window, and noticed her getting on the highway. All so subtly, I feel myself drifting in and out of this sleepiness.

Suddenly, I was in this courtyard area with endless fields, and it seemed weird that there weren't flowers. The fields were uninviting, like someone did not want any flowers to grow from them. I was scared, running as fast as my legs would let me away from a shadowed character that followed a few seconds behind me as he ran with a vengeance. While I ran, I was exasperated and nervous, and nothing was making sense. I remembered when I caught a glimpse of the shadowed man that he looked familiar, but I couldn't put my finger on it, especially in the rush I was in. I felt my heart rate increasing. I put my hands up and out, gasping for air because I felt like I couldn't do this anymore—and then I felt my friend's arm on my shoulder.

I woke up startled, and my friend, still right there next to me, squeezed my hand before asking if I had a bad dream, and I told her yes. She tells me I was gasping for air. I looked around again and the rain was slightly calmer. We were on a part of the highway that I could not recognize, either because I had never been on it or because it was too dark to make anything out. I noticed the milkshake was still in my grip and I put it to the side, and my eyes felt heavy again.

I drifted in and out, and I saw the shadowed character again. This time, he was running closer up to me, and I couldn't run anymore. We were still in a field that had no flowers. This time, I had tears rolling down my cheeks because I knew that this was the part where I ended. I started to tell him, "You don't understand why I am the way I am. When I was younger-" and my voice broke.

I tried to get the words out, but I felt another tapping on my shoulder, and I jolted awake. I woke up to my friend asking me what I was seeing and feeling. She looked worried, and I quickly touched my face, under my eyes. I felt the real tears that were streaming down during my nightmare and gasped. I told her that even in my dreams I can't find any rest for myself.

I noticed she took an exit and parked the car outside of a gas station. There were lights above every gas pump, but other than that, there were no people or any light in sight. She tells me to keep sipping so I don't fall asleep until we get back to my apartment. I decided I needed to talk to her so that I don't fall back asleep, and she talks to me, too. I wanted to talk about her, so we talked about each other, hearing each other's voices against the dark and rain.

We finally came back to my apartment, our hair soaked, and the tears rushed in again when I told her how I did not want to be an innocent flower anymore. She told me that I am more complicated than that, and people were just late to get to know me, and that I am worth the effort. I didn't have the energy to say anything at that moment, but it was a reminder again that I am lucky to have true love in my friendships. I held onto her shoulders, staining the back collar of her shirt with tears until I tired myself out and I fell asleep as she pat my back, several hours into a new day.

I fell asleep expecting a nightmare, even if it was not a continuation of the same nightmare I had felt before. Maybe it was because my friend reminded me, again, that I deserved love and dreams that I ended up having a dream instead of a nightmare. In this dream, though, I was in a vast city on an island, surrounded by water.

I was in this grocery store buying a loaf of bread and met a shadowed character outside of the store—I could tell she was a true friend, but I could not put my finger on who it was. She was excited to see me and was holding a brown paper bag with a handle herself. She asked me if I was ready, and I told her yes. We walked down this narrow strip of land, completely surrounded by blue-grey water, that led to a building of a couple of floors, and I was led to the second floor by the doorman dressed in slacks. I opened a door on the side of the floor, and it was my new safe haven. I brought the bread into my new apartment, and I stared out of one of the large windows, where the sky was slowly darkening, the lights of the city were shimmering, and my heart felt like it was glowing every time I blinked. I'm safe. I glanced over at my true friend, who was by the kitchen counter. She reached into the brown bag and pulled out a bouquet of flowers with strong, beautiful petals, and placed them on my counter.

I reached out to hold them, but I felt so much sunshine over my eyes that I jolted awake. I got up to see that it was a blissful dream, one after so many years. I looked for my true friend, but she had left.

I glanced over at my dresser and noticed the bouquet of strong-petaled flowers that she had left behind for me.

jazz club

After I realized that you were not thinking of me anymore, I barely thought of you either. Every time I started to think about you or smile at our past memories, I caught myself and cursed it off. You barely cross my mind anymore, especially when I have control over my thoughts and the places they go.

Every night, though, my control shuts down right when my eyes do, and I have been seeing you in my mind again lately. I have been waking up frustrated at first, and then it turns into anger, and then sadness—because I can't shut the thoughts of you away even when I want you out.

The nightmares are blending into my reality with you, and I am slowly becoming unable to separate them. Tonight is the sixth nightmare I've woken up from, thinking of how tomorrow will be the sixth morning that I wake up in angry tears again because it's the sixth time you entered my mind without my permission.

We were in a jazz club, the neon lights flickering on the inside and the windows exposing the heavy showers of rain that were not going to stop anytime soon. There were large orange candles at the center of each table and smoke throughout the room against the red and brown decor. I came alone because you were the only one who loved jazz as much as I did, and we've broken apart from each other's lives.

There were people performing, smoking, drinking, and laughing in the room as I was headed to my usual table all alone. I knew you were not going to perform tonight, so I felt okay coming here. I could not avoid you, though—you know where my personal table is and you left me a letter at my spot. You wrote my name on the envelope, and I could spot your handwritten scrawl from anywhere. I did not want to open this because seeing your words again was just going to open the scars I just painted over. So, I waited all night to open it, watching performance after performance. Clapping, smiling, numbing with glass after glass, and pour after pour.

The music reverberated through my body, painting over my scars again until they felt like they were finally fading. It was time to walk a few blocks home in the showers that were pouring heavier than before, but I was afraid of your letter getting soaked. I did not want to clutch it close to my chest, under my jacket, because I did not want you or your words close to my heart anymore.

I thought I would open your letter before walking into the showers because I thought I was numb enough now to take in your empty words. The letter was several pages long, longer than any talk we have ever had, and it was all nice and gentle, but it was completely empty. In the end, you say again how you cannot give me what I want. That you want to spend time with me, listen to jazz with me, but nothing more than that.

I realized I am not numb when I feel the sting of my tears coming out again and when I feel like ripping up your words that I read like a fool, letting you communicate to me again when I just want you out. Now my scars have risen to the surface again, and my whole body is stinging in frustration, anger, and sadness. I gave you yet another chance to make me feel like I was not enough for you.

The last line of your lengthy letter said you missed me, and you knew that you could find me here tonight. I realized you were sitting in the jazz club the entire night and I just did not notice you. I do not want to see you though, so I stepped towards the reddish-brown door and got ready to leave into the rain. As soon as I stepped out into the rain, I let my hair drench in the showers while my warm tears blended in and got confused with the cold rain around me.

I walked a few steps until you put your arm out and asked why I did not look for you. I looked at you in tears, saying that I already knew you liked me a little, but it was not enough for me—that I had to walk away to protect myself and quit hearing that I was not worth loving. I wanted to scream, but the words did not come out, and you pushed my wet hair from my eyes and held my chin. I threw your hand off, telling you that you would never be able to give me the words I want to hear from you.

Then you told me again, with that intense certainty I always fell for, that you think you are ready to tell me something meaningful, that you feel the same way, but you were just fighting your own scars. So, you grabbed my hand again, and you clutched tighter so I couldn't let go this time.

You bent down to ask me with certainty and intense eye contact if I would talk to you one last time. My scars always faded at your touch, so I felt like I could not do anything but say yes. You took my hand, and we disappeared into the rain together to talk again, hopefully for the last time.

The streets were empty for blocks and blocks, no people to be seen except for us, no voices to be heard except for ours. A few blocks later our conversation was the same emptiness as the letter you wrote and the conversations we have had before. Now, there was a couple in front of us sharing an umbrella, their conversation much lighter than ours.

They were close enough that we could see them walking in front of us, but far away enough that we would never reach them.

linen to living

It's always been the same day for me, but that is what I prefer. Reading and coffee in the morning, then the workday, and then dinner with my roommate before bed. On the weekends, a hike and some shopping are thrown in there. I find comfort in having a planned day and satisfaction from doing my work. I know I take no risks, and most people would think of my days as dull. I get insecure about how people might find me boring, but you only have one life, and I want to spend mine planned out.

Between our meetings, my friends at work will tell me, "You need to be louder, you need to be brighter, you need to live," and I know they mean well. What they never seem to grasp is that I genuinely enjoy feeling this way. It's not just rolling out of bed and going to work for me—I notice the chirping of the birds outside and the sun of the city shining on my face in between. It's not just drinking the same dark coffee to survive the meetings—it's the smell of the coffee beans when I wake up and the satisfaction of crossing things off my to-do list. It's the hunger after I come home and the cool air outside when I'm done with work. It's the feeling of a hot shower with my eucalyptus plant creating scented steam and then climbing off into linen sheets, knowing I have everything ready for a beautiful day tomorrow. I never considered small talking with people at work over alcohol or gambling away at a casino. I have grown to enjoy my own company, and now I prefer it to the company of most.

When I get lonely, I can drop my silence and talk to someone, but only a worthy conversation. Not a conversation traced with, "How's the weather?" and, "I'm doing well, you?" I promise I am so much more fulfilled this way. I rarely feel like breaking my routine. Last Thursday was different, though.

I woke up and decided, for one of the first times, and on my own, that my routine was not going to suffice today. I did not even consider calling in sick to work. I went to my closet and opened the lowest drawer of my dresser, the one with the clothes I always promised myself I'd grow the personality to wear soon. I look at the work outfit I had planned to wear the night before—the light grey blazer and loose satin blouse underneath. The wristwatch that reflected my place in the corporate world. I looked away before I changed my mind and grabbed some clothes from my lowest drawer. Tight, dark, and fitted. I was going to be different today.

I slip into these clothes, skip the daily straightening of my hair, and dab some deep plum lipstick onto my lips. I prance to the door and open it to the noise of the city. The world is slowly waking up, but today waking up means something different. I first take a slow walk to my favorite pastry spot, the one I only visit once a year on my birthday. I choose several slices of fluffy cake and flaky pastries and then hold them in my hand on a napkin because I do not have the patience to sit and take them in.

I walk through the city, popping into stores I had never even dared to go into before. I try on more clothes, throw them off, and buy them even if I have no idea when or where I would wear them. I walk again, without a plan, noticing the color of the sky has gone deeper. I see a bus I have never seen before, and I notice people's laughter radiating on it.

I run into the bus, throwing my loose change into the container, and run into a spot before I can hear the coins settle into the box. I'm next to so many people, strangers of the city who I have never seen and will never see again.

I make small talk with them, and I speak of the weather. It somehow leads to us sharing our hearts, and I know it does not matter because I will never meet these hearts again. I do not know where the bus is headed, and that is comforting today. Eventually, the sky begins to look the shade of midnight, and I stare outside while I eat my last pastry. It has been years since I have seen what the world looks like while I am usually asleep.

I decide to wave goodbye to the people I have talked to and leave the bus to welcome the showers of pouring midnight rain. My makeup is bleeding, rain getting caught in my hair, and lovingly slipping off my clothes.

I have no clue what time it is, where I am, or what my story tonight is going to be. I feel dangerously safe. I hear someone call me beautiful, something I have not heard in a while. I turn around, and he says, "You look like you have a story." I find myself walking towards him, hearing my heeled boots fight against the puddles of rain underneath us. "Only today," I say, walking closer to him.

He holds my cheek and our lips meet.

C

between the valleys

I was deep in my desk drawers, and I found a little box from my twenties, which might have been the best years of my life. There were a few little scraps from my travels in the box, but shining the brightest was the little flag. It was a little dowel with a delicate rectangular flag attached—a rich, navy flag with golden embroidery upon it. The embroidery had what seemed like endless rows of valleys, with trees between each valley upon the cloth and a crescent moon in the upper-left corner.

I smooth it out with my fingertips while latching, as I do often, onto the memories of my trip to the happy valleys a decade before. My sister and I were burnt out after a couple of years working away in the city and came to one of our frequent realizations that there existed corners of the world in which people just stayed still instead of quickly moving all of the time. We had this urge to visit a remote island, one that was hard to get to and hard to leave from. It was terrifying at first not knowing who our company would be or when we would return.

The urge to leave was strong, though, and we ended up wandering off the island we traveled to. Off the coast of the island were several boats supposedly going to the smaller nearby islands. Not knowing where we were going, my sister and I hopped onto one, solely based on the smiles and permission of the other two in the boat. The boat took us to the happy valleys, the most special place I have ever been or will ever go to.

We met the people of the valleys who had more in common with us than we could have ever imagined. They were so loving because the only fight they had was against the outside world that was begging them to move faster. We spent most of our days there learning the language of the happy valleys and eating strange fruit by the coast. We made friends with the few hundred others who lived in the happy valleys, learning their smiles and their stories. I could have spent days listening to their stories and laughing with the children as we picked flowers together and ran through the steep valleys.

I had spent so much time chasing the next event in the city that I could not have even imagined what it was like to slow down. I had no idea the people of the valleys had protected themselves by allowing themselves to simply be and float in the beauty around them instead of chasing task after task to worry their vast minds.

The nights were even more special, and if I close my eyes tight enough, I can see it in my mind again. Once the sun set in the happy valleys, the sky would graduate from shades of teal to shades of navy, with a few brazen reddish-violet streaks. The moon would celebrate its new phase in the sky as it rose, and there was mist in the air, protecting the now dark-green shadowy valleys under it. The trees would appear to be asleep, and you could feel the water settling if you listened closely.

The happy people of the valleys would string lights upon their houses as soon as the sun started to go down, and then the music would start. It was a specific melody that started off as light, jazzy music that caressed the entire island like a feather.

My sister and I were never able to figure out exactly where it came from, but it would start in the middle of the valleys and radiate outwards until every heart that resided in the valleys was filled with evening bliss. The music would go on, the jazz getting warmer and people singing along fading only after the birds sang their own songs to wake the island up.

I had been looking for my real pace all my life, and I found it in the happy valleys. The only thing I brought back was that navy flag, a reminder of what the nighttime mist was like between those hills.

Every night since I came back, I wondered why the people here were in such a rush instead of enjoying every phase of the moon like I had learned to. I look out the window sometimes, to look at what it looks like tonight.

I know that somewhere far away, between the happy valleys, the moon was celebrating its phase in the sky with a special jazzy melody tonight.

afterglow

We were running late on our way to the beach one night in June, and the skies were already darkening. I'm with my cousins and sister with the windows down in the car until the air feels saltier and we're there. Our shoes go into a pile in the sand, and we run, some of us hand-in-hand when we dip into the cold water.

Seeing miles of the ocean stretch so effortlessly has always me feel small, like I'm protected by something greater. It feels like there's something to hold onto or fall back on. I feel like we should have come earlier, though. We swim across the night and excitedly jump at the waves that approach and feel them hit against our skin.

An hour passes, and the sky darkens even more. Now I can barely see where the sky ends and the ocean begins. The waves crash the same regardless of how the sky is colored. It feels a little dangerous, but I am here with the right company and know that this is a new, stunning memory in the making. My hair was straightened, but the curls came back after my first dip in the ink-looking sea. Not many others are here, so all I can hear is the voice of the sea and my cousin's laughter blending in with the sky.

When the first stars start to appear and the moon begins to rise, we swim back to each other. Hand in hand, we start walking to the shore and then to the pile of our previously abandoned shoes. The grains of sand stick to our ten feet up to our ankles, as if the ocean was inviting us back in by leaving its mark on us. We get to the pile of shoes and start walking back to the car, talking about how we could have gotten better photos and had a better time if we had made it out here before sunset.

My sister realizes she left her shoes in the pile, so we wait for her to walk back to find them. A few minutes pass by, and we hear almost a hysteric scream, the kind that makes you run to its source right away. Worried, I run to her while the sand beneath my feet tries to slow me down. I reached her and tapped her shoulder from behind, asking if everything was okay. She does not look like anything bad has happened, but I can tell she has experienced something she has never experienced before.

She points to the shoreline and motions for me to glance in that direction. I have never seen anything like it before and cannot come up with an explanation. Hand-in-hand like always, we reach the shore and sit against it. Along the shoreline are what seem like millions of strange, clear beads.

They are giving off a glowy light, some of the beads shades of electric blue and some that are stark white. One of my cousins lays her hand beside the lit-up shore. It is strange but not unsettling. It feels like the ocean is glowing after we left it like no one has appreciated her for a while in the way that we did.

None of us has experienced anything like it before, but we know it has to be natural when we see it twinkle in front of us. We hold hands again and sit against the shore while we silently admire the afterglow that we almost missed.

We have been back to this beach a couple of times since then, but the ocean never glowed the way it did that day.

horizon of ink

I have these moments, especially when the sky darkens and my hopes decrease, when I feel like everything is infinitely heavier. I feel tornadoes spinning through my stomach, slowly ripping my insides out. My mind feels like it's been shocked from the inside like lightning has struck it, and I have a billion blinding thoughts while somehow feeling completely blank and numb at the same time. My skin takes turns either burning at the touch or shivering from the air it's in. My breaths and heartbeats get faster, my patience grows thinner, and I can't lie still. These moments come out of nowhere sometimes, and it feels like I am out of my body. It feels kind of like my own mind, but I cannot ever be sure if it is.

The first time I saw the sea past midnight instead of broad daylight, I felt the same way. It seemed like the sea I knew, but it was so different from how I knew it before. The sky and the sea seem like rich, liquid ink during the after-hours, blending into one another to the point where I could no longer tell them apart. It seemed natural, but it made me feel unsettled when I could not differentiate where the sky ended and the sea began. It felt like it was all the same thing, even though I knew deep inside somewhere that they were two vastly different entities.

When I have these all-consuming moments, I feel the anxiety

and reality blending into one another, the way the liquid ink seas at midnight blend into the dark horizon. The spinning thoughts make me feel like I am drowning in this liquid ink sea, and my heart becomes a tiny vessel. I feel how small my heart is when I realize that it is all I really have to help me hold every wave of this inky, endless sea.

It is despairing because my tiny vessel cannot even hold a single wave of the ocean, and I feel like I have to hold the entire midnight sea to avoid drowning in it. I usually blame the entire situation on my vessel—it has never been big enough, it has never been strong enough, it's just never been enough. Sometimes I am convinced it has holes in it.

Sometimes I feel a glow over me while I feel myself sinking, like there is a force or maybe the light of a lighthouse shining over me. It almost feels like hope, but not exactly—it's hard to have hope when I am drowning among all of these thoughts and waves, and it feels like there is no way to save myself. The light is enough for me to wonder, though, like maybe someone would hand me a much larger vessel so that I wouldn't drown.

Sometimes I wish that someone would swim over to me. Maybe they'll hand me a vessel that can hold every single wave of the ocean, and maybe they'll say, "Give all that water to me. Give all that pain to me." Maybe then I would not drown in the ink or feel out of my body.

I don't feel hopeful when it comes to getting a new vessel, though, so I keep treading because the glow feels light on my back. I always tread, even when I feel like I would rather drown.

I always tread because even though the sea and the sky blend into each other during the after-hours, I can always trust that soon, they will divide again for daybreak.

acknowledgements

Thank you to my bestest friends and family for loving me and my story always. I love you and I am the luckiest girl in the world to have you in my life. Thank you to Adrienne Kisner for editing moonrise and talking to me about liminal spaces. Thank you to Kaitlin Sclafani for reading and editing moonrise and celebrating it endlessly during every stage. Thank you to Luísa Dias for creating a cover that is straight out of my dreams and remembering to put a bow in the girl's hair. Thank you to Sathvic for believing in me everyday and every moonrise. Last but the most sweet, thank you to my cousin and best friend Divya, for telling me that my sticky note scribbles and spacey thoughts could turn into a book someday.

about the author

Hi! I'm Neha. I'm either from the Midwest or the East Coast, I don't even know anymore. I like baby pink, pumpkins, lowercase letters, and the ocean. I am an INFJ through and through. I love scribbling and have had a little bump on my right middle finger from writing too much all my life. I like putting together silly little outfits to drink coffee with my friends. I cry easily, and a lot, but I don't think it's a bad thing. I have always felt a little out of place but I think I will find my place soon. I also love blueberries.

You can follow me at:

@moonrisebyneha

Milton Keynes UK
Ingram Content Group UK Ltd.
UKHW041903120324
439302UK00005B/265